Loved by the Single Dad

The Single Dads Club

Sierra Shipley

Cover Design by Sierra Shipley

Table of Contents

Books By Sierra

The Claiming Her Series
His Temptation
His Disaster
His Reward
His Challenge

The Rose Prairie Series
All Tangled Up
Tied In Nots
It Had To Be You

Interconnected Stand Alone
Yes, Captain
Hey, Neighbor

The Single Dads Club
Loved by the Single Dad
Nanny for the Single Dad
Desired by the Single Dad

SIERRA SHIPLEY

Chapter One

Hazel

Nothing says *spring is here* more than dodging stressed-out parents while wild kids run around looking like lost puppies trying to find a soccer field. The early morning sun is warm enough to wear shorts and a tank top, but the chill in the air had me reaching for a jacket before making the trek from the car.

"The one by where the giant beehive was in that tree that one time," my sister laughs obnoxiously into the phone. "Remember? A bee started chasing you and when you ran, you tripped on a branch?"

The image of that tree and a flashback to that day pop right into my mind. "I still have a scar on my foot from where that branch cut me, you know. And that bee *did* sting me." I can't keep the amusement from my voice. Although it wasn't necessarily what I meant by "which soccer field?" it does the trick.

Wind rustles through the speaker. "Whatever you say," her voice is thick with sarcasm. "The tree isn't there anymore, but the stump's still there. Right behind the goal." I can hear Mason's breathless voice ask her a question, drawing her attention.

"Got it. Be there in a sec."

A great sense of nostalgia settles through me. Growing up, soccer was my family's lifeblood. It didn't matter that I wasn't the most athletic of my parent's three children—I still can't run to save my life—but every waking moment of Saturdays growing up was spent at the soccer complex.

I wonder if players still get free popcorn and soda after a game.

Families walk side-by-side, grandparents carry mugs of coffee and maps of the complex, while over-prepared soccer moms drag wagons of stuff behind them with their husbands trailing after them with their noses in their phones. None of them bother paying attention to me as I weave in and out of the unnecessary traffic.

It's never fun walking into the complex alone, but I'm used to it by now. My brother's daughter Betty has played for several seasons, but today is Mason's big debut and I'm all for showing my support.

The crowds get thinner the farther into the complex I walk. Fresh footprints leave marks in the dew-speckled grass, the scent of spring filling my nostrils. There's something about the soft scent of wet grass and fresh, cool air that's comforting.

I take a moment in all the chaos around me to enjoy it. The spring sun warms my skin and I angle my face up to soak up the rays letting my eyes slip closed as I walk. Red paints my eyelids making me think of long road trips. I suck in a relaxing breath just as the world shifts. Like a slow-motion shootout scene from a movie, the bright sky streaks by in a blur as I brace myself for impact.

"Shit!" I hiss as quietly as possible because I know I'll get hateful looks from uptight parents if they hear the words spill from my mouth. The muscles and tendons of my ankle give way, buckling and rolling underneath me. My hot pink lawn chair slides off my shoulder as I lose my balance, smacking me on the shin as I throw my arms out to brace my fall. I bite my lip, my eyes squeezing closed against the onslaught of pain.

By some form of torture, I'm the klutziest person I know. If there's a single hole in an otherwise hole-less field, my foot will find it. Unfortunately, this isn't the first time I've found myself in this exact predicament, calf deep in a hole.

Heat flames my freckled skin in pain and embarrassment. I'm just happy I didn't fall to the ground and that my ankle is one piece.

There's a distinct and all too familiar throbbing sensation centered around my twisted ankle, and I know there's no way I'm making it out of this hole unscathed.

No big deal. This sort of thing happens all the time. Surely, I'm not the only person to have ever twisted their ankle in this same exact hole, right?

Trying to look as unfazed as possible with a bruising shin and throbbing ankle, I readjust my chair strap over my shoulder and hobble—hopefully in the right direction— to my nephew's game.

The longer I walk the more pronounced my limp becomes. By the time I see my sister my ankle is swollen, my shin is pink and bruised and I look like I need a pair of crutches.

Rounding the corner of the field, Candice sees me limping toward her. "Hazel?" Her eyes go wide with concern. "What happened?"

"Oh, just another hole. I'm fine. Nothing I can't handle." I brush her concern aside, removing my chair from its sling and setting it next to hers. The ground is soft from recent rains, and I can feel the chair sink as I settle into it.

"At least let me look at it." Candice is way more maternal than me. She's the kind of mom full of hugs, kisses, and motherly affection.

Even though I don't have kids, I'm not sure I'm cut out for it. All the mothering genes went straight to my sister. My style would be more hands-off. Bleeding? Go play. Get up, brush it off—you'll be fine.

She stands before crouching down in front of me. "Which ankle is it this time?"

I bend down and point to my swollen left ankle. "Really? It's the size of a watermelon and you ask which one it is?" I laugh.

"I didn't want to assume. For all I know, your ankle is always this big." She smiles up at me, her eyes crinkling as she does. Her hands are cold as she gently examines my injury. "I think it's just twisted."

"I could've told you that," I reply, my voice thick with sarcasm.

She ignores me and pushes herself up. "We should probably put some ice on it. Where's Tony?" She scans the field for her husband, but he's nowhere to be seen. "Wait here."

"Like I have anywhere to go," I mumble as she walks away.

While waiting for Candice to return from wherever she took off to, I watch my nephew run around as he warms up for his game. It's his first year playing soccer and he's been bouncing with excitement for weeks that he's finally playing. He's been watching games with his dad since he was born, and I have a feeling he's going to be a natural.

Not gonna lie, these kids are freaking cute. The little boys on the team are adorable in their matching uniforms and socks that cover half of their little legs. One player's shirt swamps him, hanging down to his knees as he runs to the sidelines presumably to get his uniform tucked in.

"I've got ice coming." Candice sits in her chair next to me adjusting her ball cap. We've got the same shade of dark auburn hair, but hers is more manageable in every sense of the word. Sleek, shiny, and short, her low ponytail tickles the collar of her jacket.

We're exact opposites, her and I. She's graceful and lean, while I trip over the air and have abundant curves. Straight hair to my wild wavy tresses that I can barely keep contained on a good day. She's nurture and I'm nature. Ying versus yang or whatever.

"Thanks. You didn't have to."

She waves me off. "What're big sisters for?"

We catch up on our week as we wait for the game to start while watching Mason run in excited circles around the field. I got here earlier than I thought and I'm enjoying the time I get to chat with my sister.

She teaches nursing courses at Liberty College in Briar Springs, is the president of the PTA, and hosts a monthly book club. I swear, I've never seen her relax, but she always has the best stories.

"Someone needed ice?" A man's voice pulls us from our conversation, and I raise my hand like I'm still in school.

"That would be me," I say, still a tad embarrassed by the fact that I can't seem to walk without harming myself. The mid-day sun makes it hard to see the man walking towards me. He's cast in shadow, the sun shining behind him making him nothing more than an outline.

"I've got a bag right here," he says, holding the zip-lock bag of ice. Shielding my eyes I look up at him. He's young, probably around my age, with a tattoo inked on his upper arm, the dark edge peeking out beneath the hem of his sleeve. He looks like he works out, his long legs toned in his shorts. Aviator glasses frame his eyes but they do nothing to block his kind smile.

"Thank you so much. I'm such a klutz, but you should see the other guy. No," I rush, after he quirks an eyebrow, "there isn't another guy. I'm all alone. So alone. It was a hole. My foot. I stepped in it. Not on purpose, of course. Accidentally." I don't know why I'm telling him all this, but I can't seem to stop myself. "You're my hero," I say, taking the ice he offers and biting my lip to keep myself from spewing another damn word.

What am I saying?

"Twisted ankle?" He asks, and I nod trying to get the bag to stay put on my gigantic ankle. He gestures towards my foot. "Mind if I take a look?"

Fully aware of the word vomit I spewed, I try to keep my answer as short as possible. "Go for it."

He squats in front of me and now I'm able to get an up close and personal look at him. And damn it, he's just my type. Tall, tan, lean, and ruggedly handsome. The sun highlights his light brown hair making it look blonde. He slides his sunglasses off his face as he examines my swelling appendage. "We should get this ankle in the air. Let me go get my cooler and we'll be all set."

"Oh, no. I'm fine," I stammer. "This isn't my first rodeo," I joke.

"Mine either," he says, and I swear he winks. It was probably the sun catching his eye before he slid his sunglasses back on, I'm almost sure of it. "I'll be back."

And damn it, I watch him walk away, admiring his tight-looking ass. Which is totally inappropriate given we're at a kid's soccer game. Not the time or the place.

"Um, Candice?" I lean over and tap my sister's arm to get her attention the moment he's far from earshot.

"Hmmm?" She's busy looking at her phone, probably texting her husband to find out where he is.

"Who's that?" I ask.

"Who?" The man in question slips between a set of parents and my gaze slips over to her where I give her my best *really?* look. "Oh, that's Grant. He's Mason's soccer coach."

Hello coach.

I've *got* to tell Jo about this. A cloud blocks the sun momentarily shading us as I pull out my phone to tell my best friend how hot my nephew's coach is. "I wish my soccer coaches looked like that growing up," I say to myself as my fingers type frantically in our text thread.

"Ahem."

Oh, come on.

It wasn't a cloud that was blocking out the sun. It was Grant. And he heard every damn word I said.

How embarrassing.

"Ankle up." He places the cooler in front of me, completely ignoring my comment. Maybe he didn't even hear me.

Thank. God.

He gently helps me lift my ankle, gingerly setting it atop the cooler before reaching forward and picking the bag of ice off my lap where I left it.

"Thanks," I say as a sharp whistle blows. Grant double-checks the placement of the ice before giving me a quick nod and jogging onto the field.

Crisis averted.

Now I have more things to tell Jo, but that can wait 'til later.

Watching little kids play soccer for the first time is entertaining. They all trail after the ball like little ducklings. The boys take turns kicking the ball in any direction except toward the goal. As much fun as it is, I find myself distracted most of the game, too busy checking Grant out instead of watching my nephew.

What is it about seeing a man with kids that makes him seem a thousand times more attractive? I mean, he could be an average Joe, but the minute he hugs a crying five-year-old?

Boom ovaries explode.

By some miracle, Mason managed to score three goals by the end of the game. He must have a never-ending source of energy because even after chasing the ball for the entire game he still has enough energy to run laps. I have no idea how my sister puts up with it all.

Confined to my chair, I watch Candice pass out snacks to Mason's teammates. I could start packing up my chair, but with the pain in my ankle now a dull thrum, I might as well sit here a bit longer before walking back to the car.

A cute little boy with dark blonde hair stands in front of me, orange pulp caked across his cheeks as I watch my nephew run in circles. He turns, looking behind him before saying, "Hey, Daddy? I want my juice, but this lady has her foot on it."

Daddy?

Grant comes jogging over, a warm smile on his face. "Just a moment, bud," he says to his son as he ruffles his hair. "How's the ankle?"

I slide my foot off his cooler a little embarrassed that I didn't figure out that Grant has a kid. Of course, he would have a kid. You don't see childless men coaching soccer. That'd be weird.

"I'll survive." I smile back at him. "Thank you again. You didn't have to do that." I try to hide my cringe of pain as my foot hits the ground.

"You're welcome. I'm a sucker for a damsel in distress, especially one that compliments me."

So *now* he wants to acknowledge what I said? Great.

I force a polite laugh, dying on the inside. "I'll let you have your cooler back." Everyone around us is packing up so it's time to put my ankle to the test. Bracing my weight on my uninjured leg, I stand. To my surprise, it's not as painful as I thought it would be. I'll still be a gimp but walking back to the car shouldn't be too much of a hardship.

Grant holds his hands at my side almost like he's worried I'll topple over, poised and ready to catch me if I should fall. "Are you good to walk?"

"All good." I focus on keeping my mouth shut. The last thing I need right now is to embarrass myself even further than I already have.

The cute little boy digs around in the cooler and pulls out a bottle of Gatorade. "Dad, can you open this?" He holds it up to his father expectantly with the sweetest look on his face.

Ugh. It's too cute.

I start packing up my chair, hoping no one sees the indentations in the soft ground where my seat has started to sink.

"Auntie Haze!" Mason's dark hair weaves through the dispersing crowd coming right for me. He looks more like his dad with his golden skin, dark eyes, and black hair. The freckles though, he gets from his mom, and me by default since it's the only other thing we seem to have in common.

Mason takes a running leap and I'm barely able to drop my chair as he flings himself in my arms. "I scored so many times! Did you see me?" I kiss his sweaty temple and squeeze him tight hiding my wince of pain as I put our combined weight on my uninjured leg.

"I sure did. Are you sure you're only five? You looked like a pro out there."

He giggles and shakes his head. "You're silly, Auntie Haze."

"I know," I chuckle, squeezing him one more time before setting him back on the ground. Mason is my favorite little boy in the whole world. He's also the only little boy I know, but whatever.

Tony finally appears and helps Candice grab all their chairs, throwing them over his shoulder as we head to the parking lot.

"Where have you been? I didn't see you at all." My eyes are glued to the ground, keeping an eye out for possible danger zones, my chair bouncing against my hip with each wobbling step.

"I was at the bench helping the other dads." He says it like it makes complete sense.

"Oh, I didn't tell you!" Candice leans around her husband to look at me. "They have some sort of dads club thing going on. They all hang out during practices."

"Really?"

"It's cute, actually," she admits.

Tony huffs. "It's not a club and it's not cute."

"It's okay, baby. Whatever you say," she cajoles, patting his arm before turning her attention back to me. "They're all hot too."

"Really, honey? I'm right here," Tony cuts in, but she ignores him.

"And they're single," she adds with a wink.

For as long as I can remember, Candice has been trying to set me up. First, it was with a co-worker who was so odd it made me question her judgment. Yes, I might be a single twenty-eight-year-old, but I have to draw the line somewhere. Then, there was the friend-of-a-friend situation that I'd like to forget. "Ha, if you're playing matchmaker, I'll pass."

Besides, why would I want to be paired up with one of them, when I couldn't take my eyes off Grant? Plus, there's *no way* he's single. Not to mention that he wouldn't even be interested in me if he was.

They never are.

Chapter Two

Grant

The birthday party is packed with children running wild and screaming. I'm just happy Harrison happens to be one of them and isn't throwing a fit like he was fifteen minutes ago.

Wells and I watch Tristan and Harrison run around the large backyard with their friends. The entire team was invited and they've been talking about this party all week.

"Anyone want a two-year-old?" Cole comes to a stop in front of us looking like he's had one helluva rough morning. His energetic daughter, Marie, is wiggling in his arms struggling to get loose and screeching like a bird in the process.

I feel for my friend. It's not easy parenting one child, let alone two. Cole's been through the wringer with his contentious divorce and the mother of his children moving across the country to be with her new boyfriend, leaving Cole with sole custody.

He sets his youngest down on the grassy lawn and she takes off like a rocket, running off to join the bigger kids as Cole tells his oldest son, Jett, to keep an eye on her.

"How do you guys do it?" Cole asks, his expression wary. His normally put-together appearance is ruffled this morning, his shirt wrinkled and face unshaven. It must've been a worse morning than I thought.

Wells chuckles, crossing his arms. "For starters, I only have one." Wells's son Tristan is a tiny little guy. His soccer jersey hangs off his small frame almost to his ankles, even now his clothes swamp him, but that doesn't stop his spunk. "And I wouldn't say I'm a pro at it either. Not like Grant is."

"Oh bullshit," I scoff. "You only see the good parts. My morning was probably similar to yours," I admit. Harrison was a little monster this morning. He woke up at five, spilled milk all over the floor, and refused to get dressed for Mason's party. He threw a fit the whole way here and only stopped crying when he saw the bouncy castle and cake.

I almost did the oldest trick in the book and threatened to turn the car around.

Across the chaotic backyard, Tony spots us and walks towards us, grill tongs in hand. "Hey, guys. Thanks for coming."

"Dude, I'd do anything to get my kids out of the house," Cole jokes, but the desperation is clear in his voice.

Wells slaps Tony on the arm. "Thanks for inviting us." Handshakes are exchanged with the host before a small ahem has us looking around our circle. A mess of brown waves glistens in the sun immediately catching my attention.

"Um, I was told to bring you guys some drinks." She shrugs, gesturing down to her arms loaded with cans.

It's her. The woman from Harrison's game last week. The one with the swollen ankle that I haven't been able to get out of my mind. She's absolutely stunning and I can't help but gape at her.

"Thanks." Tony grabs a can from her, popping the tab, the hiss of the carbonation ringing out. He takes a sip before making introductions. "Hazel, this is Cole, Grant, and Wells. Hazel's my sister-in-law."

"Ah," she smiles. "The infamous club." Her cheeks flush slightly, making the freckles dotting her nose and cheeks stand out even more.

"Club?" Cole asks as he takes a can from her.

Tony sighs, muttering under his breath, "Not this again."

"The Single Dads Club," she states matter-of-factly. We all gape at her, completely dumbfounded. "You know, you guys have formed a little club for soccer practice. I heard it's a tough club to get into, sorry Tony." The cans in her arms jostle, growing slick from the condensation.

"Here," I offer, reaching toward her full arms, "I can take those." Her soft skin brushes against my fingers and the contact isn't enough.

I want more.

"Oh my gosh, thank you. These things are freezing." Her arms are speckled red from the cool aluminum of the cans, and I can't stop my eyes from raking up and down her body.

Hazel has luscious, mouthwatering curves that I find irresistible. I noticed her last week from across the complex while Harrison warmed up. She was limping, but I couldn't take my eyes off her. Her legs looked smooth as silk in her denim shorts, and her breasts bounced distractingly in her tank top with each step. When I heard Candice asking around for ice, I didn't hesitate.

"How's the ankle?" I'm dying to have a conversation with her. Wells, Cole, and Tony are talking amongst themselves and aren't paying any attention to me.

"You remembered," she says, looking surprised.

As if I could forget her.

"I never forget a patient," I tell her, and it's true. I've been a pediatrician for several years and always remember a patient. Especially not one that looks like her.

"Well, then I'm honored." For a second I think her ankle gives out again before I realize she's curtsying. Her eyes widen and pink darkens her cheeks as if she realizes what she did. It's so damn cute that I can't help but smile at her, earning a smile back. We're grinning like fools at each other while a mob of children runs around us. "I'm completely healed, as you can see." She points her left leg like a ballerina, and sure enough, her ankle is back to a normal size. Not even a hint of a bruise.

My gaze locks on her shapely legs, blood rushing to a place not appropriate to mention at a kid's party.

It's not often that I find myself enamored with a woman, especially after the mess of Harrison's mom. But there's something about Hazel...

I've been single since the moment I became a dad, and it's worked out well for me. Work and unexpected fatherhood took control of my life and if it wasn't for the men standing beside me right now, I'm not sure where we'd be.

Hazel's smile falters as her eyes dart around the yard as if looking for someone. "Is your wife here?" Her voice is no longer fun and playful but has a nervous quality to it.

"How could I be part of your infamous club if I had a wife?" I tease.

Her shoulders shrug, her wild waves slipping over her shoulder. "I could have some bad information. '*The Possibly Single Dads Club*' doesn't have the same ring to it. Plus, my sister is known to be misinformed." Hazel laughs as if recalling a specific incident.

The noise of the party falls away as I look at her. Her warm-toned skin seems to glow from within radiating through every pore that it escapes from her rich brown eyes. Freckles dot across her entire face, flitting across the bridge of her nose to both cheeks. And that smile? It makes me want to wrap her in my arms and never let her go.

"Honestly, I'm surprised by that. Would've thought you'd been snatched up by now." She playfully nudges my bicep, her eyes shining with amusement.

If she only knew what that simple touch was doing to me.

The only person I want to snatch me up right now is her. "What about you?" I ask before my imagination gets the best of me.

For all I know, she could be married or have a boyfriend and I don't want to get my hopes up. The jealousy at the thought is hard to ignore.

"Me?" She laughs dismissively. "Nah, I've got no one." She says it like it's always been that way and will always be that way.

Not if I have something to say about it.

Little hands pull on my shorts before I can ask her more about it. "Daddy?" My son's light green eyes gaze up at me expectantly.

"Harrison, I'd like for you to meet Hazel. She's Mason's aunt." His little eyes dart over toward her where she smiles softly and waves.

"Hi," his little voice chirps before he turns right back to me. "Daddy come jump with me." When I don't respond he quickly adds, "Please?" in that way, which makes it impossible to say no.

I look over to Hazel who smiles politely. "It was great talking with you, Grant," she says before waving and walking away.

Her hips sway with each step away from me, and I can't take my eyes off her.

An insistent tugging of my hand breaks my stupor. "C'mon, son. Let's go bounce." I pluck Harrison off the ground, tossing him over my shoulder as he squeals with laughter.

Chapter Three

Hazel

Part of me thinks I made a fool of myself with Grant, while the other part says, who cares? I'm a single woman and I'm not going to let anything hold me back. Besides, what've I got to lose? Sure, it could make for some awkward soccer games for the rest of Mason's season, but then I could never see him again for the rest of my life. No harm done.

Past me would've never batted an eye in Grant's direction because there was no shot he would look at me. Now? Well, he still might not look at me, but why not take that chance?

It's taken a lot of personal growth to get to this point. When you don't look like the other women in your life, your mind plays some games on you. I was gifted with large curves that I can't decide if I want to accentuate or hide. Nothing like the slim, athletic build my sister inherited from our mother. But there's no changing the width of my hips, and there's no changing if someone is attracted to me.

Like with every woman, there's a distinct love-hate relationship with my body. It's a thin line separated only by my attitude of the day. What I love one day quickly becomes horrendous the next with a single thought. But after years of trying to tamper down those swings, most days are relatively the same.

It's my body and I'm happy with the way it looks.

For the most part.

I'm not sure which kind of day it is today. I was feeling all sexy and confident in what I call my suck-in leggings—because they hold in all the jiggly bits—and my tunic shirt. But since I've been helping Candice set everything up for Mason's party, I'm sure my makeup's now smeared, and my hair's a frizzy mess.

God, no wonder Grant looked happy to be getting pulled away by his adorable kid. I look like Medusa's step-sister. But... There was a moment back there where I thought he was staring at me, and not in horror like my hair was about to eat his face. I sigh, brushing said hair off my sweaty neck. He likes me or he doesn't. How am I supposed to know?

After twenty-eight years on this earth, it's safe to say that I, Hazel Elizabeth Bryant, am a terrible dater. I've been on many dates, some set up by friends or God forbid, my sister, but they always go wrong. I can think the date went well, that we were flowing and having a good time only to end up ghosted. It's happened more than once, I might add.

Which is why I've given up on the idea of love. What's that phrase Shakespeare wrote?

Love is rude and pricks like thorns.

Dating may not be love, but fuck does it prick.

So now I don't bother. But something about today and Grant that made me think, for one moment, that love might be coming my way.

Guess I was wrong.

All afternoon, I can't seem to stop scanning the yard for Grant. There was one time when our eyes met, making me think he was doing the same.

It's all in my head, right?

Mason's having an absolute blast. He invited every kid he knew to this party and from the looks of it, everyone showed up. The kid's got piles of presents and Candice had to run to the store to grab more hotdogs. Tony manned the grill all afternoon and was occasionally accompanied by one of the Single Dads Club members.

"You think we're ready to deal with this hotdog mess?" Candice looks about as flustered as I am. There's only so much planning that can go into a party before you have to fly by the seat of your pants, and boy are we flying.

The picnic tables on their deck are covered with chips, condiments, and salads that are more for the adults than the kids. We've tried to be mindful of different dietary restrictions and made sure to have a variety, but that's only added more stress.

I survey the spread with my hands on my hips. "I think it's as good as it's going to get at this point. It's better to feed them now before they turn into hungry little monsters."

Candice chuckles. "Yeah, you're right." She takes one last long look at the tables before heading to the top of the steps. "Excuse me, everyone," she cups her mouth with both hands and shouts over the excited screams of all the kids below. "Hot dogs are ready and there are tables up on the deck with chips and things."

Tony lets out a loud, "Let's eat!" and people chuckle as they move toward the grill to get their hotdogs.

As much as I think I want a family of my own, it's days like this that make me glad it's just me. The amount of stress this whole thing has put on Candice has me breathing a sigh of relief that I don't have to mess with it. All the stories of waking up to vomit-soaked sheets, nights of zero sleep, poop fiascos, booger bombs, and walking into crazy messes make me thankful for my quiet, single life.

Sometimes though, when I'm laying in bed all alone thinking about how I want my life to play out, I think I want something different than what I already have. Then a terrible sinking feeling hits me right in the chest and my thoughts screech as they make a lightning-quick u-turn.

Parents and kids bump into each other as they take their seats on the deck, children grabbing food with their grubby little hands and being general messes. The organized plan Candice and I had in mind plunges it into chaos.

Arms reach. Fingers snatch. The food scene from *Hook* comes to mind as all the little kids snatch food off platters and plates left and right.

A giant crash has everyone freezing in their tracks. In all the bumping and jostling, a bowl full of potato chips managed to get knocked off the table, the grease-smeared chips littering the deck like confetti. After a split-second pause, everyone goes back to their food, completely ignoring the spill.

Of course.

With a sigh, I walk into the kitchen grabbing the broom before returning outside. In the minute it took for me to go inside and come back, people ignored the spill and walked right over it.

Sometimes, I hate people.

With an exasperated sigh, I grip the broom, ready to clean up after the ungrateful guests. But a warm hand on the small of my back startles me.

"Let me get this." Whipping my head around, I come face to face with Grant. His crystal blue eyes mesmerize me, momentarily shutting off all brain functions.

"W-what?" I stutter, overwhelmed at how close he is. He's inches away from me, his hand on my waist as he reaches for the broom. And God, does he smell so good.

"You've been busy setting everything up. The least I can do is clean up this mess." He gently takes the broom from my frozen fingers. "Go sit and eat. You deserve to rest a bit." His eyes are kind and crinkle a bit in the corners.

"It's okay, I can handle this," I say as I reach for the broom.

"Are you always this stubborn?"

"Maybe. It's a high probability."

He chuckles at that, his laughter sparking goosebumps. "You're something else, aren't you?" His voice has a sense of wonder to it, but I could just be reading into things.

"So I've been told," I retort. He doesn't give in, even as I playfully tug on the broom handle. Grant holds fast, his eyes squinting in focus. We have a momentary broom standoff, each of us refusing to back down before I give in. "Fine." I release the handle. "You win this time."

"Thank you," he grins, full of triumph at his victory. "You go eat while I do this. Relax a bit."

"You better be prepared for next time, 'cause I won't back down as easily."

He's already started to sweep the potato crumbs into a neat pile, laughing at my challenge. "Oh, I don't doubt it. I look forward to our next competition."

Damn him and those twinkling blue eyes.

Time to walk away, Hazel. Leave the man alone.

My stomach chooses this moment to growl as loud as possible. Grant underestimated how stubborn I can be. The only real thing that could get me to back down from a challenge is hunger, and I'm downright starving.

I weave my way through the crowd stopping when I get to Grill Master Tony. "Please tell me you have some left?" I lean against the small table next to him and peer at the hot grill, praying even a morsel is left.

Tony chuckles at my discomfort but quickly assuages any concern. "Don't worry. I set a couple aside for you and Candice. I wouldn't forget about two of my favorite people."

Sometimes I forget I've known Tony for more than half my life. He and Candice started dating when I was a pre-teen. He saw me through all my awkward pre-pubescent stages that teenagers nowadays don't seem to have. "Oh, thank God for you, Tony. I could kiss you."

His face scrunches in a look of horror. "Please don't."

Laughter bubbles from my throat at his expression. I only meant it as a joke, but he looks scared that I'll actually do it. "You might have to keep one eye open," I tease playfully as he puts two hotdogs on my plate.

"I'm not worried, I'll sick my club on you. They'll cover my back."

"Ha! Please do. I wouldn't mind that one bit." I don't think any girl would turn down Wells, Cole, or Grant. Those men are sexy as hell.

"Go eat before I tell Candice."

"Ooh, I'm so scared," I say, my back to him as I head up the deck steps to scrounge for some bottom-of-the-barrel chips. Honestly, I think she'd agree with me.

26

MASON'S GASPS AS HE opens presents are hilarious. I mean, I think he's the most hilarious kid I've ever been around, but admittedly, I'm biased.

"I always wanted one of these!" Mason holds up his new favorite toy that he probably has never seen before taking it out of the wrapping paper. "It's so cool!" The children gathered on the lawn in front of him ooh and aww right on cue. It's too damn cute.

I'm standing off to the side underneath the giant oak tree that makes Candice and Tony's backyard nice and cool during the summer. My smile grows as I watch my nephew open his many presents, each one garnering the same reaction that seems ever-present today. Tears sting in my eyes just thinking about how big he's getting and that soon he's going to be too cool for his Auntie Haze.

"You okay?" Grant's deep voice rings from behind me, making me startle.

I blink rapidly in an attempt to help the now-forming tears evaporate faster. I'm not sure how it works, but it does. "Oh, yeah. Stuff like this makes me emotional," I admit. "I'll get over it."

"Ah, stuff... Presents?" He's trying to make me feel better and it's kind of working.

"Yes, presents," I laugh, thankful for the distraction.

Grant leans against the tree behind me so close that my skin prickles with awareness. "But seriously, are you okay?" His voice is soft and warm making me want to close my eyes and listen to him speak all day.

"Yeah." I wave him off. "I just got to thinking how big he's getting, and boom, waterworks."

Crying isn't something I do often, or at all, really. Every once in a while, a dog video or stress overload has me blubbering, but on the day-to-day, nothing tends to phase me.

Mason opens another present, the same shock and joy painted on his face, and for a moment, Grant and I stand side by side in contented silence watching the show before us.

"Hazel," Grant's deep voice is soft, drawing my gaze to him. "Can I ask you a question?"

"Go for it." Butterflies erupt in my belly at his closeness. There's something behind his gaze that is making me shiver in anticipation.

He sucks in a large breath, setting me even more on edge with every second that passes. "I'd like to take you out sometime. Would you like to go on a date?"

Oh my gosh, it's happening.

It's not all in my imagination.

My face shows every thought and there's no stopping the cheek-splitting grin that takes over my face. "Of course." My heart is racing, and I feel breathless, but fireworks are going off right now.

Grant smiles back at me, and we're both grinning fools, but I don't care. This might be my chance to be the girl that gets picked.

Chapter Four

Hazel

"**D**o you come here often?" I walk to the edge of the platform peering down at the expanse of green below. "I've heard that people love it, but I've never done it myself." The unmistakable sounds of clubs whishing through the air followed by the thwack of golf balls echo all around me.

This is our third date and each one gets better and better. On our first date, he took us to the park near the college campus complete with an expertly packed picnic basket. When he tried to get me to walk across a field in my wedges though, I had to remind him of how we met. The man simply turned around and gave me a piggyback ride. I don't think I've ever been swept off my feet before.

Literally.

We watched the sunset enjoying each other's company. With the tension between us, I thought I was going to combust. When he finally cupped my jaw, leaned in close, and asked to kiss me, I thought I was going to die right there and go to heaven. But then his lips met mine and brought me back to life.

After that first date, Grant followed up the very next day. I shouldn't say I was shocked because he told me he would, but to have someone follow through for a second date was refreshing.

It took a while, but I convinced him it was my turn to sweep him off his feet. Unfortunately for me, Iron Drive is so much more fun than our trip to the aquarium. Although making out in the jellyfish room with the changing LED lights is something I'm not likely to forget anytime soon.

Or making out at my doorstep.

God, I sound like a horny high schooler.

"Oh yeah, I come here all the time."

I bend over placing the golf ball on the rubber stand. "Really?" Satisfied that the ball won't roll off after several failed attempts I adjust my feet and swivel my hips. I have no idea what I'm doing, but I'm pretty sure this is how the pros do it.

Grant chuckles. "No."

My crazy hair whips in my face, my stance forgotten as I look over my shoulder at him. "Seriously?" I laugh.

Grant looks impeccable under the dull glow of the overhead lights. The sleeves of his black button-up are rolled up to his elbows showing off tanned forearms that have me drooling. He's left the top two buttons undone showing a tempting sliver of his chest. A dazzling smile shows off the sharp angle of his clean-shaven jaw helping to bring out the crinkle of his blue eyes.

He steps toward me, his chest brushing against my back as he takes hold of the golf club. His lips brush against my ear, goosebumps prickling my skin as he breathes, "I just wanted an excuse to wrap my arms around you."

I swear I've short-circuited.

Trying to play it cool and act like I didn't just soak my panties, I chuckle leaning back against his warm hold. "Just letting you know, you don't need an excuse to do that. I'm more than happy to stay right here."

He hums in my ear before placing a kiss on my neck. "I can make that happen."

"Unless we want to get kicked out for indecent exposure, you should probably help me hit the ball. It'd be embarrassing to have to call my sister to bail us out of jail."

Out of all the dates I've had in my life, none of them compare to Grant in many ways. He's far and away from all of them in how he treats me and makes me feel. I don't think I've ever had this strong of an attraction to a person. Both physically and mentally.

"We wouldn't want that."

Despite him never coming here, he knows what he's doing. He sets up my stance, adjusting my hips and fixing my grip. The whole time he chats about learning how to golf with his dad and hopes to teach his son someday. "Now bring the club up like this," his hands cover mine showing me the proper swing of the club, "and hit the ball."

"Ha! You make it sound so easy."

He steps back safely away from the swing zone oozing utter confidence in me. "You've got this."

"Okay," I mutter under my breath. "Don't miss the ball. Eye on the prize. Swing and don't miss."

"Any day now, Hazel."

My gaze flicks between the ball and the giant expanse before me. "You can't rush perfection." I appreciate that he doesn't snicker behind me, letting me focus.

Sucking in a large breath, I loosen my death grip on the club, pull my arms back, and swing.

Eyes glued to the white ball resting at my feet, a surge of pride swells as it moves from its precarious perch from the sheer force of my swing.

It's too bad I miss the ball entirely.

I must've loosened my grip too much because the only thing that goes flying towards the green is the club.

All I hear is my shocked gasp and Grant's stifled laughter as I stand frozen, my fingers poised around a grip that's no longer there. I'm not sure whether I should shout *'fore!'* or *'watch out!'* but nothing comes out.

Stunned, I slowly walk to the ledge and peer down praying the wayward golf club didn't take out an innocent bystander. All the air deflates from my lungs as I tentatively scoot a toe to the edge.

There, resting in the safety net lining the edge is the club I inadvertently threw.

A second set of shoes comes to a stop beside mine. "I think I messed up," I say softly, still in shock. When my gaze flickers over to Grant's, I can't stop the laugh that bubbles from my throat.

"I think you need more coaching," he says after our laughter dies down.

"I think you're right. It's a good thing I have you then."

After having an attendant fish out the club, Grant works with me in between taking his swings. And if I'm honest, I might be pretending not to understand how to hit the ball. He's a good coach and is patient taking me through the steps, but it shouldn't take ten tries to learn how to swing. I'm not sure if he caught on, but I don't think either of us minds his hands on my body.

In between my lessons, I enjoy watching Grant's powerful body twist with each swing. His shirt stretches over his shoulders hugging the curve of his back as he holds his pose following the path of the ball.

We might have to make a return visit because I could watch him all day.

When I manage to hit the ball, he sweeps me up in an enthusiastic hug, lifting my feet off the ground and spinning me around. I never thought I'd have someone pick me up once, let alone twice, but it's thrilling. After giving me a piggyback ride through the park on our picnic date, I've learned to not question Grant's strength. Plus, I very much like the feeling of being in his arms.

Both tired from our driving practice, we decided to head into the cozy bar area. I watch as he walks over to the bar relishing the thought that he's here with *me*. He catches me staring and winks.

Everything about our dates is different from anything I've experienced before. Nothing has felt awkward or uncomfortable. It all feels so natural. Right.

"How in the world are you single?" I ask, thanking him for the mojito. I'd assume he'd order a beer, but his drink's the same as mine.

Grant sits across from me, bringing the drink to his mouth, his eyes piercing into me. "I could ask you the same thing."

I give him a flirty smile. "I asked you first."

Grant leans forward resting his elbows on the small table. The flickering candle between us makes it seem like we're the only two people in the room. "I think it's obvious."

"Not to me."

He glances down at his drink, spinning it on the wooden tabletop. "Women aren't pounding down a single dad's door these days." He pauses, giving me an adorable nervous smile. "I wasn't exactly prepared to be a father."

"Is anyone?" I ask with a chuckle.

"I guess not. But when a baby shows up on your door from your ex-girlfriend who you didn't know was pregnant when you broke up, I'd say that's as unprepared as it gets. Dating was something that got put on the back burner."

Well, now I feel like an asshole.

Obviously, I knew he was a single dad basically from the time I met him, I just never imagined how he got there. Now it makes sense.

"You didn't know?"

He shakes his head. "Things with Julie were...difficult. We were together several months before it was clear we weren't going to work. I was just starting my residency and was living in a run-down apartment. Then nine months later I woke up to desperate knocking to find a newborn Harrison in his carseat. He was a couple of days old. He didn't even have a name yet. The papers shoved next to him in his blanket said 'baby Rollins' along with legal paperwork with the dissolution of Julie's parental rights."

My mouth involuntarily pops open. I can't imagine how difficult that must've been, how shocking and terrifying it was to go through that. How does anyone handle a situation like that? The man in front of me casually sipping his drink has to be one of the strongest people I've met. One of the most solid.

I try to work the shocked expression off my face. "And she was just gone?"

He sucks in a deep breath. "Yeah. I've been single ever since. Raising a newborn and working my residency was more of a struggle than I ever anticipated. My parents, Cole, and Wells helped when they could, but dating was out of the question. It's gotten easier since I started the private practice, but I haven't found anyone who's caught my eye quite like you."

Butterflies take flight in my stomach. I love how open and honest he's being about his past and about me. It's not the typical metaphorical chess match the first rounds of dates tend to be.

"You know," I say leaning forward, "you have to be the most amazing person I've met." And I mean it. Every other guy I've dated hasn't come close to the character and integrity of the man across from me.

Grant smiles, laughing softly. "I doubt that. You never got the chance to meet you," he counters.

"Me?" I scoff. "I'm just a normal girl."

"Yes, you. I don't know how I got so lucky." He says it so matter-of-factly that it's hard to argue with him. Grant leans over the table and I meet him halfway. The kiss is soft, gentle, and lingering. Our lips part before he smiles at me. "Don't think you're going to get out of answering by distracting me."

"And what question was that again?" He honestly kissed the crap out of me and I can't remember anything from the last several minutes.

"Nice try," he chuckles. "How are you single?"

The chilled alcohol cools my chest as I take a drink. "If I knew the answer, I'd tell you." He watches me intently, urging me on. "I swear."

His blue eyes squint playfully. "How do I not believe that?"

"It's true," I say with full sincerity. "I've never been lucky in love. Try as I might, it's been a futile endeavor." He gives me that look that all men seem to master that means *go on*, so I do. "Candice was the one that the boys flocked to. I was the girl on the side." Grant visibly jolts back. "No!" I laugh. "Not like that. What kind of girl do you think I am? I mean, the wallflower type. There, but not standing out. When I got older and went to college I blossomed and embraced who I am. Then..." I suck air through my teeth, shrugging. "I've gone on countless first dates, but nothing's stuck."

Grant's eyes lock on mine in the dim candlelight making everything seem more intimate than it is. Without breaking his gaze he holds up his drink, the ice clinking softly as he holds it up between us. "Until Now."

"Until now," I add with a shy smile, lifting my glass to his with a soft tap.

THE GLOW OF THE SIDEWALK lights illuminate the dark lawn outside of my apartment complex. Grant's car idles at the curb, the engine purring softly, its gentle vibrations matching the anxious feeling in my chest. I don't want to get out of the car and it seems like he doesn't want me to go either based on his firm grip on my knee. His pinky rests just underneath the hem of my summer dress, and something about it has my heart pounding.

"Here we are," I say breathlessly.

Fingers skate along the skin of my thigh. "Here we are."

We linger in silence as the tension between us builds. I never imagined that I'd have such a connection with someone like this. I want to learn everything about him and jump his bones at the same time. It feels like I've won the lottery. I've had three of the best dates of my life with this handsome, caring, giving man.

I swallow hard pushing through the haze of sexual tension. "I guess I should go inside now." I reach for the handle but a tight squeeze on my thigh pauses my movement.

"Wait."

"Yeah?"

Blue eyes burn into mine. "I can't let you go without a kiss first."

I smile. "I was hoping you'd say that."

Grant doesn't hesitate, unbuckling his seatbelt and reaching for me across the console. A hand caresses my jaw before sliding into my hair pulling my face softly towards his.

A ragged breath leaves my mouth before his lips connect with mine. I'm putty in his hands, molding my body against him the best I can in such tight quarters. I'm holding him to me, melting around him as he draws me closer to him.

When his tongue slips through my parted lips I moan, my panties dampening with each teasing touch. Grant hums against me as the heat builds. So slowly the hand locked on my knee trails steadily up my thigh and if I could form coherent words, I'd beg him to move faster.

Grant pulls back, breathing heavily as his fingers brush against the fabric of my panties. Wordlessly, I spread my thighs in enthusiastic consent.

A possessive hum rumbles through his chest setting off a wave of desire and I pull his mouth back to mine in a messy kiss. My hands curl into fists around the buttons of his shirt as he slips his fingers inside my panties.

The breath rushes from my lungs with his gentle yet determined exploration of my folds. My chest heaves with ragged breaths as he kisses his way down my neck, sinking his fingers into my wetness.

"Hazel," he groans into the crook of my neck working his fingers in and out of my pussy.

Sweat covers my skin like dew. I'm on fire for him, my skin burning, overheating. It's all too much and not enough.

My head falls against the leather headrest letting my body sink into the seat, lifting my hips to give him better access. I need him everywhere. Need to feel him everywhere.

"Please don't stop," I whimper in the silence.

Grant's mouth finds mine stoking the flames of desire lapping at my skin. "Never."

The pad of his thumb slowly circles my swollen clit as he continues to pump his fingers slowly in and out of me. I'm so wet for him that the evidence of my desire is making obscene noises that I might be embarrassed by if Grant didn't hiss in satisfaction.

Everything fades away. The hum of the engine, the leather creaks of the seat as my hips rock against his hand, the fact that we're in a car parked on the curb. Nothing except the musk of his skin, the brush of his lips, and the feel of his fingers.

Small moans become more clipped with each stroke, each brush of his thumb. My fingers sink into his hair as the pleasure builds until it's almost too much.

Hot breath brushes my face and my eyes slide open to meet Grants. He curls his fingers and adds more pressure on my clit, his gaze never leaving mine as he pushes me over the edge.

Pleasure radiates, pulsing through me like a battering ram. His mouth drowns out my cries of pleasure, the thumb of his free hand stroking along my jaw in utter adoration as my heartbeat slowly steadies.

Grant kisses me softly before slipping his fingers from my core leaving me feeling empty without his touch.

"I can't believe we just did that," I say, my limbs like jello. I feel like a naughty teenager letting my boyfriend finger me before sneaking into the house after curfew.

Grant chuckles as he rights my skirt making sure I'm carefully covered. "Oh, I can. You've just made this car my favorite place." He leans over for a quick kiss before sighing. "Can I walk you to your door?"

There's no missing the very noticeable bulge in his pants and I try not to stare. "Absolutely."

All I want to do is drag him inside and finish what we started. Instead, Grant's a gentleman and walks me back to my first-floor apartment.

"Would you like to come inside?" By inside, I mean 'round two' and he knows it. I lean against my door pulling him to me with both hands.

Grant obliges, wrapping his arms around my hips and kissing me. The bulge that I definitely stared at earlier, now pressing against me making my heart hammer with anticipation. He groans. "I promise you, I want nothing more, but I have to go pick up Harrison."

Oh. Right.

I try to keep the disappointment off my face. He's got a son to take care of, a responsibility I can't understand. But I can understand his decision.

I sigh, resting my head on his chest, breathing him in. "I had fun tonight."

Soft lips brush the top of my head as he hugs me tight. "Me too." He kisses my lips once more before releasing me. "Sleep well. I'll call you tomorrow."

He waits until I unlock my door, his hands in his pockets like he has to hold back from reaching for me. The bright smile he gives me before I shut the door warms my heart. And as I tuck myself into bed, my smile and that feeling of warmth don't fade.

Chapter Five

Grant

All four kids run around Cole's backyard with full bellies and happy smiles. This isn't the life I imagined when I graduated medical school, but nights like this make me realize all the hardships were worth it.

Every Sunday night we meet up at Cole's house for dinner. We tried rotating between our houses, but Cole's is by far the nicest. His backyard is the perfect setup with a large green yard with a playset for the kids and a covered patio with a TV mounted above the built-in fireplace. The kids can wear themselves out while we watch football or baseball, or whatever is on.

Now if only Hazel were sitting in my lap, things would be perfect.

Thinking of her has me hiding the grin that pops on my face whenever she crosses my mind, which is often, especially after the other night. The whole drive to Wells' house was spent trying to calm my raging erection. It didn't help that every time I looked at the empty seat next to me, I'd remember Hazel melting at my touch.

"What's got you lookin' like that?" Cole kicks my foot off the coffee table to nudge his way past me before plopping on the couch.

"I don't know what you're talking about."

Wells leans forward pointing the neck of his beer bottle at me. "It's the same look you had the other night when you picked Harrison up."

"Whoa, whoa, whoa." Cole sits up. "What am I missing here?"

"Yeah, Grant. What are we missing?" Wells usually isn't the shit-stirrer, but tonight's my lucky night.

My two best friends glance at each other before fixing back on me. They're not going to let me get away with not telling them about Hazel. I didn't tell Wells why I needed a babysitter Friday night and my parents don't ask questions when I need them to watch Harrison.

"Look, I've got nothing to say." I hold out my hands to protest my innocence, but they're not buying it.

"Like hell, you do," Cole laughs. "I've known you for a helluva long time and you're hiding something."

"Time to tell us about the woman whose perfume you came home smelling like." Wells leans cockily back in his seat knowing he opened up a metaphorical highway for Cole to exploit.

I rub my forehead at the headache I feel coming. "Here we go."

Cole leans forward, all business. "Oh, a woman? Is it one of those handsy moms at the office?"

I laugh in denial. "Seriously? What are you, a teenager?"

Cole squints his eyes as he stares at me ignoring my comment. "You didn't tell us, so I'm thinking it's someone we know. Who has he talked to recently?" he shoots his intimidating gaze over to Wells.

"How the hell am I supposed to know?" Wells snorts.

A squeal of pain has all three of us sitting up, our attention turning to the lawn. The three older boys stand in a group looking guilty as Marie turns her tear-filled eyes to her dad and wails from the ground.

"Boys!" The sound of Cole's voice has all three boys looking at the ground.

"This is all you," Wells adds before taking another drink as Cole makes his way to his daughter and to deal with our guilty sons.

Grateful that something more important than my love life has their attention, I breathe a sigh of relief.

A chorus of arguments rings out from the yard drawing a sigh from Wells. Our sons are like brothers and they sure as hell fight like 'em. It's clear they're willing to blame anyone as long as they avoid punishment. What they haven't seemed to figure out yet is that they'll get punished no matter what.

Cole comes back, Marie resting her head on his shoulder, her hiccups making her whole body shake. "Our sons decided to play keep away and smacked Marie in the face with the ball. They've had a stern talking to. One of you can dole out punishment." He lowers himself into the chair with an exhausted sigh. Apparently, it's been a long weekend at Cole's house.

The seven of us are our own family, chosen and forged through years of friendships and challenges. It doesn't matter who gives the punishment, the two men beside me are my team.

Right on cue, all three boys step onto the concrete porch looking at their feet.

"Take a seat, boys." With scrunched-up faces, they take a seat on the couch next to me in three different stages of anger and guilt. As if a flip is switched the moment they sit down, all three start up the argument they began on the lawn. Jett's quick to throw the blame on Tristan, who says it was Harrison's idea to play keep away.

It gives me a headache thinking about what they'll be like in ten years.

All it takes to get them to stop arguing is a whimper from Marie. The one thing they can all agree on is that Marie got hurt because of their actions.

After five minutes of disgruntled silence, the boys say their apologies, clean up their discarded plates, and get back to playing. Marie stays in her father's arms fighting sleep with dark circles under her eyes.

"So who is she?" Cole's like a dog with a bone and he isn't going to let go easily. It's what makes him a good lawyer, but a pain in the ass to keep a secret from.

Wells snorts knowing that I'm not getting out of it.

"Her name's Hazel." Saying her name has her face popping into my head.

Cole's face scrunches. "Why is that familiar?"

"She's the girl from the birthday party," Wells says matter-of-factly. "Tony's sister-in-law, right?"

"The one who called us that club. What'd she call it?" His fingers tap against the arm of the chair. "The single dad's club. She's right," he chuckles, "it has a ring to it."

The smile on my face is involuntary.

"Well, we're happy for you. It's about time one of us gets back into the dating pool. Five years is a long time." The faraway look in Wells' eyes is unmistakable. Five years might be a long time, but to him? At times it seems like yesterday.

"She's special, I feel it."

"She have any friends?" Cole jokes. "Wells looks like he could use a night out." Cole ignores the middle finger flipped in his direction with a snort.

"I think you should be more focused on finding a nanny than worrying about me," Wells shoots back.

The three of us laugh, the conversation about my relationship with Hazel pushed to the back burner as we fall back into familiar territory.

"How's work going? Things picking up?" A sweaty Harrison crawls into my lap, water bottle sloshing as he brings it to his lips.

Wells' landscaping business is starting to hit the busy point of the season and he's constantly on the job. After the frigid winter temperatures, people are bursting at the seams to make their lawns beautiful again.

"It's starting to get that way. Remind me that I'll need to do something for myself before the summer ends. Drag me out if you have to."

During the spring and summer months, we're lucky to see him at all. Of course, we still have our get-togethers and hang out with the kids, but he's fully committed to his business during the rush times. I swear he doesn't let loose often enough despite our prodding.

"We'll hold you to that." Marie sighs in Cole's lap, her little mouth clucking as sleep starts to drag her under. "I've gotta go get this one ready for bed." With a huff, Cole pushes out of the chair and heads for the door.

"Yeah, we should get going too." Harrison issues a drawn-out complaint, but he has school tomorrow and if he doesn't get enough sleep, he'll be cranky in the morning.

"Us too," Wells says, ruffling his son's hair as he whines, his little shoulders slumping.

With a final goodbye and a round of hugs for the boys, we're finally home for the night. Harrison doesn't complain when it's bath time and is fast asleep in no time.

Me, on the other hand? I can't stop thinking about Hazel. She's been on my mind all day. What would it be like to spend a lazy Sunday morning cuddling on the couch and drinking coffee while Harrison watched cartoons? Even something as mundane as grocery shopping would be magical if she was there.

It's an odd feeling to be thinking of what someone else is doing with their day. Is she having a good day or does she need a hug? I've only had Harrison and myself to keep my mind occupied and I find adding Hazel into the mix has been effortless.

We texted earlier in the day—she was going to brunch with some friends—and I haven't heard from her the rest of the day.

I need to fix that.

Rolling over in my bed, I check the time and decide it's not too late to call her. If it is, I'll face the consequences later. Right now, I just need to hear her voice.

My head rests on my pillow, my hair rumpled in my reflection on the screen of my phone. If I'm gonna get in trouble for waking her up, I might as well get a chance to see her face, so I opt for a video call instead. Nervously I clear my throat hoping she answers.

"Hello?"

Hearing her rough voice makes me laugh. "Did I wake you?" Her wild hair is piled in a bun with several loose strands framing her face. The smile on her face will make any anger worth it.

"No," she sits up, the camera shifting to the sound of ruffling sheets, "I was reading on my phone."

I don't know what I was expecting when she popped on the screen, but the satin gold spaghetti strap sleep top that's barely there has my heart thundering out of my chest. How did I get so lucky?

"Good. I'm glad I didn't wake you, but I needed to see you. Hear your voice."

"Oh," she says playfully with the raise of an eyebrow, "Is this one of those booty calls? I always wanted to get one of those."

"Seriously?" I laugh, grinning like a fool.

Hazel's eyes squint adorably as she giggles. "No."

How have I lived thirty years without having her in my life?

I arch my eyebrows playfully. "We could make it one if we wanted to." I'd much rather have my hands all over her, but I'll do anything for her.

She narrows her eyes at me. "Oh really?"

"Yeah. I wouldn't mind getting a repeat of the other night, even if I don't get to touch you."

She tries to hide it, but her breath hitches. "Don't tempt me. I might have to get out of bed and sneak over to your house, which would be hard considering I don't know where you live, but I could do it." Instead, she does the opposite, sinking under her covers and laying her head on her pillow.

Why am I constantly smiling around her?

"I believe you could." I agree as she pulls her blanket up to her chin. "We can save that for another time."

And there will be another time.

"Thanks," she says through a yawn.

"Sorry, I shouldn't have called this late. I'll let you sleep."

"No," she rushes, sitting up so quickly the blankets slip down her torso making my heart hammer once again. "Don't hang up. I like talking to you."

"Okay." A sense of calming happiness settles in my chest. "What do you want to talk about?"

A relieved expression flits across her face as she lowers herself back to her bed. "Hmmm..." She taps her chin. "Why did you become a pediatrician?"

"Wow, you're wanting to fall asleep fast, huh?" She issues a soft disagreement, urging me to continue. "My grandpa was my favorite person in the world growing up. He was a pediatrician for forty years. I'd go to his office after school until my parents got off of work. He'd let me mess with all sorts of stuff, usually getting myself into trouble in the process." I snort at the memory. "I think all that time seeing him with his patients and spending time in his office wore off on me. He said his proudest day was when I graduated med school."

"I love that story. It sounds like he loves you."

I sigh. "He did. I wish he would've been able to meet Harrison. He would've loved meeting the great-grandson who's named after him."

Hazel's voice is soft. "I'm sorry."

Grandpa Harrison died three weeks after my graduation. Knowing I made him proud in his final weeks keeps me going to this day. Absently, I reach across my chest with my free hand to rub the caduceus tattoo I got in his honor on my arm. "How was brunch?" The dull light of her bedroom makes her freckles stand out and I wish I was there with her to kiss each one of them.

"It was good. Maybe you feel this way when you meet up with Cole and Wells, but life seems easier when Jo's around." I nod. No matter what, when they're around, everything's good. "She's super busy downtown at her corporate office and barely has any free time. The older we get the harder it is to find a time to meet up. I'm lucky she can carve out a slot for Sunday brunch."

That's why we have a designated night where all three of us hang out. Between Wells' busy season, Cole constantly running around like a chicken with his head cut off, and me with the practice and coaching, it feels like time hardly slows down.

But carving out time for Hazel? That's effortless.

"I'm glad you got to see her."

"Oh me too. Plus, she loved hearing all about you and the Single Dads Club." Her eyes sparkle with mischief.

I shake my head, smiling. "You and your names."

"What?" she asks, mock offended. "Someone needs to know I somehow managed to catch your eye."

There it is again, that note of disbelief that tinges her words at times. "Hazel," I say soft and low, "I hope you know I'm not planning on going anywhere."

The sudden serious turn in the tone of our conversation has her blinking in confusion. "What?"

Here we are, miles apart and talking on a video call, not at all how I envisioned having this conversation. "You think I'd let a woman like you hobble into my life and let her go? I think you'll have a hard time getting rid of me."

Hazel blows a raspberry with her lips, laughing at herself and the day we met. "Is this your way of telling me that I'm your girlfriend?" A smile spreads across her beautiful face, her teeth biting into her thick lower lip as if to stifle the same giddy feeling that's bubbling under my skin.

"God, I want to kiss you right now."

"I'll take that as a yes." She laughs. "Too bad we decided to save the booty call 'til later." Her voice has turned sultry and my body immediately responds to it.

I groan, dragging a hand down my face. "If you don't want me sprinting across town to your apartment, we better talk about something else."

"I mean, I don't *not* want that," my eyes snap open, meeting hers through the screen, "but I'll be good."

We spend hours on the phone talking about anything and everything.

"Mark's...Mark," she sighs. "He's always done his own thing, ran on his own clock kind of thing. I'd say he was the wild child."

"Really? Why did I think that was you?" We'd already gone over my life as an only child. It was nice sharing stories about my grandparents and hearing her laugh at my family's camping fiascos.

"Me?" She chuckles. "No, that was Mark. Candice is the perfect one, and I'm... well, I don't know which one I am."

We're both lying down, our phones resting on our pillows. It's like she's lying in bed right next to me and I can't wait for the day when she is. "I'd say you're pretty fucking perfect."

"Not compared to Candice." Gone is the playful tone from several seconds ago. Even her eyes, tired as they are, lose some of their sparkle.

Sheets rustle as I sit up wanting to hear her every word. "What do you mean?"

Hazel sucks in a deep, hitching breath, her eyes darting to the ceiling. "Candice is amazing and I love her, but she does everything *right*. Not only that, she's so *fucking good* at it too. Do you know how many things she does? She teaches nursing courses at Liberty College, is president of the PTA, hosts book club, sits on the city council," she ticks off the lists on her fingers. "Not to mention that she's like, the best mom in the entire world and Mason is the luckiest kid to have her. Lord knows how Tony managed to snatch her up," she mutters. "I think I better remind him how good he has it before he forgets."

She inhales, swallowing before she continues. "I guess growing up it's easy to notice how we were different. And the older we got the more stark those differences became. I don't have everything figured out like she seems to, and I tend to mess up a lot."

I wait until she relaxes back into her mattress before I do the same. "Can I tell you something?"

The soft smile she gives me has warmth spreading in my chest. "Yes."

"I think you're amazing, Hazel Elizabeth Bryant."

By the time I wish her a good night, I don't want to end the call. She's everything I've ever wanted and then some. I never imagined that I'd find the woman of my dreams at my son's soccer game, but the way I'm feeling right now, I think I have.

Chapter Six

Hazel

Grant's coming over tonight. We've continued our nightly video calls and I don't even care that I wake up exhausted. I guess that's what happens when you find yourself falling in love.

I'm falling in love with him.

Wow.

I feel like I'm at the top of the rollercoaster, all the anticipation building, the feelings swirling and growing within before I tip over the precipice.

It's thrilling and absolutely terrifying.

I've managed to stay away from love, or rather, it's stayed away from me. It's all so unfamiliar.

But the thing that's swirling in my gut? Yeah, that's nervousness about tonight.

Our nightly talks have become filled with more sexual tension than I thought was possible through a screen. Close to that dirty *NSYNC song my sister and I would listen to in secret so our parents wouldn't find out, but not quite. As tempting as it is—and it's so fucking tempting—I want to save that until we can be together.

With both of our busy schedules, we haven't been able to go on another date. He's been helping Wells with Tristan, and I've had to stay late at work for a project.

But that doesn't mean I haven't seen him. For the three weeks we've gone without a date, I've seen him every Saturday morning at Mason's soccer games.

After our initial introduction at the birthday party, Grant doesn't want to come on too strong with Harrison, and I agree. But it's hard to watch his tan skin glisten in the sunlight as he coaches the team, trying not to smile when he glances my way and winks.

Him, those blue eyes, and those mesmerizing winks are going to be the death of me. I very well could drop dead of a heart palpitation if he keeps it up. Then again, that could mean some mouth-to-mouth resuscitation...

Candice gives me strange looks, her eyebrows arching inquisitively, but I don't give anything away. I'm a sealed vault.

Tonight can't happen soon enough. If it doesn't I'm likely to combust. Grant's made sure that Harrison's at Cole's for the night and that means we have the whole night to ourselves.

This time, as we walk to my door, I know he's coming inside. His hand squeezes my waist, tucking me closer under his arm as he leads us down the sidewalk through the complex. "I missed spending time with you." He pulls me closer, kissing the side of my head. "This is the best part of my week."

Somehow he always knows what to say to make me feel like the most important person in the world.

We reach my apartment and Grant holds onto my hips as I unlock my door making my pulse thrum distractingly. I can't get us inside fast enough.

"Do you want something to drink or—" Grant grabs me and drowns out my question with his lips. I guess he's feeling as desperate for this as I am.

A surprised gasp morphs into a moan. His hands are all over me, fists clenched around the fabric of my dress as he pushes me against the wall with a thud. "All I need is you," he growls against my skin before taking my mouth once more.

Grant worships me as he trails kisses along my skin, heat blooming where his lips touch. I'm just as ravenous for him, running my hands up and down his body longing to feel his skin against mine. "Grant." I don't know if I'm begging or demanding.

He smiles against my collarbone, kissing it lightly. "Hazel?"

"You're driving me crazy." I throw my head back thumping against the wall with a dull thud.

"You don't think you've been driving me crazy every Saturday? You look like a dream. So beautiful it's distracting. The way your hair glows in the sunlight, your cheeks flushed pink from the heat. Seeing you and not touching you is madness." He runs his hands over my curves, cupping my breasts, his thumbs rubbing over my nipples making them peak through the thin fabric. "I think it's time I drive you wild, don't you think?"

"You—"

I'm left dumbfounded as Grant lifts me, my legs wrapping around his hips. Pinned between him and the wall, I'm at his mercy.

His mouth brushes across every inch of exposed skin stealing my breath. Strong fingers dig into my ass tilting my hips to the perfect angle as he grinds against me. I cling to him, my eyes rolling with each toying thrust. All the playful banter and rising tension have left me on edge for weeks and I'm damn near ready to explode.

Hot breath traces along my neck. "You have no idea what you do to me." The deep, rugged rumble of his voice sends a tingle down my spine leading straight between my thighs.

I can do little but moan against him, begging him for more. He continues to rock his hips against mine, using only enough pressure to drive me crazy without sending me over the edge. "Please," I beg, my nails dragging down his back.

Hungry blue eyes meet mine as he brushes my wild hair from my face. "Have you had enough?"

"No." I pull his mouth down to mine, making him groan. "I want more."

So much more.

He searches my gaze before adjusting his grip and carrying me into my bedroom, gently placing me on the bed.

"I think," I manage between heated breaths, "you did it. You're driving me crazy." My body's thrumming with arousal, wound up from his teasing. I can barely think past the pounding between my legs as Grant pulls down the straps of my dress and nibbles on my sensitive skin. "You win," I concede, running my hands through his hair as he exposes my breasts, taking the tips into his mouth and making me gasp. "I'm thoroughly crazed now."

He laughs before blowing air across my wet skin making it prickle. "I'm far past teasing you. I've been dreaming of having you spread out underneath me since the moment I saw you. I'm going to take my time."

So slowly he peels off our clothes making sure to kiss, touch, and caress every inch of my body.

He's every bit as gorgeous as I knew he'd be. I run my hands up and down his smooth arms, over his shoulders, and down his chest. He stands before me in perfect control as my hands wander lower over his hips until I wrap my hands around him. I watch his face, captivated by the way his eyes slip closed and how he moans so low, the breath rushing from his lungs. Seeing his reaction to my touch, I understand why he's taking his time with me.

He doesn't let me explore for long before pushing me back down on the mattress and settling between my spread legs. "You have no idea how long I've wanted to be between these thighs." Grant's hot breath skates over my sex, his voice deep and sexy. "I've been dying to taste you." He flicks his blue gaze up my rounded stomach before he lowers his mouth to the apex of my thighs.

My hips buck against his exploring tongue and I moan with each languid stroke. Grant lifts one leg over his shoulder pushing my other thigh against the mattress, opening me up for his exploration.

He's setting every nerve ending on fire, bringing me close to the edge again and again without pushing me over it. It's maddening.

"Grant, please," I whimper, twisting my fingers in his hair. "I need you inside me."

He gives me one long lick before lifting his head. "I love hearing you beg for my cock. Beg more."

He latches his mouth to my clit making me cry out. "Oh, god. Please. I want your cock."

He hums against my clit before kissing my thigh and sitting up. Grant's all lean muscles and I can't take my eyes off him as he grabs a condom and rips the package open with his teeth.

No unplanned pregnancy here. At least one of us has our wits about them because all I can think about is him and what he'll feel like buried deep in my body.

Grant lays down, rolling the condom over his impressive length. "Come here."

With an order like that, I'm not hesitating. He grabs my hips in his firm grip pulling me to straddle him. "So bossy," I tease, my lips brushing against his mouth.

"How's this for bossy?" A hand tugs at the hair at the base of my neck as he slides his cock through my slick folds, teasing me without pushing into me. "You're going to ride me until you come. You think you can handle that?"

I moan. "Yes."

"Good." He strokes one last time before his grip loosens to let me rise up on my knees.

And sink down.

We both groan with every inch. Hot breath and panted whispers of praise ricochet off my overheated skin. Sweat glistens on his mouth-watering chest and I'm tempted to lick it off of him, but my senses are on overload. Filled to the brim, my eyes slip closed relishing in the feeling of him inside me.

"Fuck, Hazel," Grant grits out, brushing wayward hair from my face. "You feel amazing."

"You're one to talk," I pant, circling my hips and moaning at the pleasure with each stroke. "I love how you feel inside me."

I've been dying for this moment for weeks now, and now that it's here, I don't want to take my time. We've been dancing around the sexual chemistry between us and I'm ready to go to full throttle.

Gripping his strong shoulders I rise up and sink back down. His steady hands squeeze my hips guiding me down as his surge upward, hitting deeper and deeper each time.

We're so close, our bodies melded together in this moment. I've never felt this close to someone both mentally and physically. He's defied everything and shows his dedication in the brush of his hand, in the hint of a smile.

I love him.

Grant's torn through every notion of love I've grown to believe. He's proving me wrong because, with him, I feel what love is supposed to be like. I've heard somewhere that love isn't how often you say it, but how much you prove it to be true, and with every action, Grant proves it.

I'm lost in the feeling of him, in this golden warmth radiating from my chest as I stare into his blue eyes that I never want to stop looking into.

"You're so beautiful. Look at you," he says as if he's in awe of me. As if I'm the most beautiful thing he's ever seen.

"Don't stop," I pant, never breaking his gaze. I never want him to stop being the man that he is. I never want to know what it's like to be without him, without his touch, his everything.

Suddenly, Grant changes our position, flipping me onto my back before continuing to thrust into me at a brutal pace

In our new position, Grant uses his hands to roam my body, teasing my nipples with deft fingers, his lips grazing over my heated skin to suck on my neck, my lips.

I do the same, touching and caressing the curve of his shoulders, his hips, and the flex of his ass as he pushes into me.

He's working magic on my body, slowly and steadily stoking the pleasure beginning to thrum through my body with each stroke. My breath hitches, "Grant."

"Let me hear you." His teeth sink into the sensitive skin of my shoulder adding to my billowing pleasure.

One cry blends into another as he finally pushes me over the edge, my walls fluttering around him, pulsating as my muscles spasm.

Grant doesn't stop, his cock hitting a sensitive spot over and over again making me see stars as I come undone.

"So... Beautiful." Then with one final push, he moans my name as he finds his pleasure.

I'm not sure how long we lay together curled in each other's arms, but it could last forever and I'd never tire of it. In his embrace, I've felt the peace that comes in the quiet moments with someone you love.

Because I'm in love with him.

How one moment in time can be the thing that pushes my feelings over the edge seems cliche, but I can't deny it.

"Grant?" My soft whisper sounds overly loud in the still quiet around us. His heartbeat echoes in my ears, his arms wrapping tighter around me.

"Hazel."

I've never said something this serious before and nerves threaten to silence me. "I think I'm in love with you." The barely whispered words seem to hang in the air and with each passing second, my heart falls.

Grant inhales, my head rising on his chest as he does and I prepare myself for the worst. I guess I've taken all those Facebook posts of '*tell someone you love when you love them before it's too late*' to heart.

"Good."

Good?

Yep, I should've kept my big mouth shut.

Trying to keep the hurt expression from showing. Fear, rejection, and humiliation sweep through me like ice water. I sit up eying the man beneath me. "Good? That's all you have to say?" I'm not expecting him to reciprocate, but damn, he could say something, anything else.

Grant cups my jaw, his thumb skating over my lip. "Hazel, I've been in love with you since you curtsied at that birthday party." He laughs softly at my stunned expression, his eyes crinkling in that way that I love. "Maybe even before then when I saw you hobbling to the soccer field."

I can't stop the smile slowly spreading across my face. "What?"

He chuckles brushing hair from my face. "Hazel," he says softly before kissing my lips. "I." Kiss. "Love." Kiss. "You."

Excitement swirls through me as I throw myself back into his arms effectively ending our conversation.

Chapter Seven

Grant

Harrison sprints down the sidewalk to the playground leaving me behind in his dust. Cole likes to think Jett's the wild child of the bunch, but Harrison picks and chooses when to behave, and today he's all wild.

I watch closely as he reaches the large wooden castle waiting for him to pop up in one of the windows. This park is our favorite which is why I brought Hazel here for our first date. From where I'm standing, I can see the tree where we had our picnic and our first kiss.

I'm already planning a return visit.

Harrison calls down to me from the tower, his head barely high enough to look over the edge and I wave up at him before he takes off to play. Which is fine with me because now I can be on the lookout for Hazel.

We set up this playdate with Mason to help Harrison get used to the idea of Hazel being around. He sees her in passing at his soccer games, but we try to keep a low profile until we can formally introduce them. The only woman he's had in his life is his grandmother and I don't want to force Hazel on him. If I have a say in it, she'll be sticking around for the foreseeable future.

I've never been happier than when I'm with her. It's fresh and new and exciting, not to mention, sexy. Whenever I can, I make sure to spend time with her much to Cole and Wells' delight. They have fun teasing me when I drop Harrison off for the night, but I know they're happy for me. And maybe a little jealous.

Hazel's black sedan pulls into the parking lot and already my chest warms at the sight of her. She doesn't see me watching her as she opens the back door to let her nephew out. A loving smile spreads across her face before she laughs at something her nephew says, grabbing his hand and walking through the parking lot.

Hazel's the most beautiful woman I've ever seen. Even as she picks hair caught in the corner of her mouth, she's stunning.

God, I love her.

"Daddy! Mason's here!" Harrison runs to the middle of the bridge clutching the railing to keep his balance as it wobbles and points to his friend across the park. His dark blonde hair, similar to my own, shines in the mid-morning sun. We picked a Saturday with no soccer games to make the most of our time together and for her and Harrison to get to know each other.

I've been looking forward to spending time with the two people I love the most. Daydreams are about to turn into reality and I couldn't be happier.

"You better get down and go greet him," I call up to him, loving his excitement. By the time he makes it down, I'm waiting at the gate, one eye on Harrison and the other fixed on Hazel.

The gate opens with a creak as Harrison pushes through it running full force toward them. "Hi, Mason. Want to play?"

Hazel chuckles as her nephew pulls his hand from hers. "Someone's excited to see you, Mase."

Someone else is excited to see his aunt.

"Harrison, you remember Hazel, Mason's aunt?" My son glances up at her with a polite smile and quiet 'hi' before both boys run off into the playground. "Well," I chuckle, "that went well."

She sighs as I wrap my arm around her shoulder pulling her close. "It's good like this. We've got all day to spend time getting to know each other."

"I know." Her hair smells faintly of fruit and coconut as I breathe her in before planting a soft kiss on her head. I want to do more, to hold her tight and press my lips against hers, but I won't. I can't. Not right now anyway.

Later, I promise myself.

"Auntie Haze! Come push me!"

Hazel laughs, patting my chest before stepping out of my embrace. "Alright, Mase. You ready to touch the sky?"

The time we spend at the park is full of fun and laughter, both from the boys and from us. Hazel's great with the boys, practically glowing as she plays with them. Harrison warms up to her, grabbing her hand as we play hide-and-seek.

Seeing her with my son like this, seeing her around children, has me dreaming of what our future together would be like. Family dinners, Christmas mornings, Hazel glowing as she cradles our growing child in her belly.

I want it all.

With her.

Since becoming a single father on top of trying to start a career, I never let myself imagine sharing a life with someone else. A love life was the last thing on my mind.

Until her.

Watching her now as she makes sure her nephew is buckled in the backseat, I can't stop the desire for her. My eyes linger on her round ass and I force myself to keep my hands at my side.

The door closes with a muted thud. "We're all set." Wind spreads its fingers through her messy curls, drawing it across her face in an unpredictable pattern. "I knew I should've worn this up. I never learn." She opens the front door, smiling as she brushes her hair aside.

I reach across the space between us catching the wayward strands and brushing them away from her face before tucking what I can behind her ears. "I like seeing your hair all wild and crazy. I think it's sexy." My wink earns a smile.

"Yeah, well that makes one of us."

It's time for her to go but I don't want her to leave. No amount of time with her is ever enough. "Thank you for today. I'm glad the boys had fun."

Those brown eyes focus on my face before flicking down to my lips. "I had fun too."

God, I want to kiss her.

"Come over later." I make sure to keep my voice low, careful of the listening ears in the backseat. Having her this close all day and not being able to touch her is driving me crazy. After the other night, she knows exactly just how much.

Hazel laughs softly. "You're not sick of me yet?"

Temptation gets the best of me and I reach up to brush her cheek with my thumb. "Never."

"HE'S OUT FOR THE NIGHT."

It's been hours since the park and Harrison could barely stay awake, his face drooping into his mac-n-cheese. He's been asleep for at least an hour and once he's asleep, he won't wake up 'til morning.

"I know that look." Hazel leans back into the couch with a hint of mischief in her eyes. She's sitting in the corner of the sectional looking like she belongs there.

Belongs *here*.

"What look?" she asks innocently, batting her beautiful eyes. "I'm not looking at you any sort of way."

I cage her against the back of the couch. "Mmhm." She tilts her head back, offering her lips as I lean down to kiss her. All the feelings I pushed back for her come flooding in and I deepen the kiss, desperately needing her. She hums in the back of her throat as my tongue brushes against hers.

Hazel slides down on the couch, lying down without breaking contact and I settle between her spread thighs. Her small hands slip under the waist of my pants gripping my hardening cock. My head falls to the crook of her shoulder barely able to contain my moan. "If you keep doing that, I don't think I'll be able to control myself," I warn her as she slides her hand up and down my length.

Hot breath tickles my ear as she whispers, "That's the plan."

Whatever restraint I have left melts away. With fumbling hands, I push her shirt up exposing her round breasts and teasing her nipples to peaks with my teeth. Her head digs into the cushion of the couch, her grip on my cock loosening as I drag ragged moans from her.

She wanted me untethered, that's what she's going to get.

She's managed to get my pants unbuttoned to give herself more room to maneuver, but it gives me the opening I need. Hazel gasps as I pin her hands above her head, my free hand slipping under the stretchy fabric of her leggings to cup her pussy.

She moans before biting her lip, her eyes popping open. "Wait," she gasps, and I freeze, afraid I've done something wrong. "Should we go to your room?" Her voice is a whisper.

I shake my head sucking her nipple into my mouth.

"W-what about Harrison?"

The sound of my son's name brings me up short. "That kid sleeps like a rock. If we're quiet, we won't wake him."

She shakes her head. "Let's go to your room anyway. I don't want to risk that chance of traumatizing your son."

As much as I don't want to stop, she has a point. "You're right." I adjust her shirt before standing, helping her off the couch, and scooping her into my arms. Hazel lets out a whispered hiss of laughter and I've never been happier in my life. With her in my arms, her body pressed against mine, nothing else matters.

My steps pause with the gentle stroke of her hand along my jaw. "I love you." My heart stops every time she utters those three words.

"I love you, too."

Safely behind the closed—and locked—bedroom door, I lay her on the bed ready to pick up where we left off. With determined fingers, I slip my hands under her top pulling it up until she's exposed for me. Her hands do the same, sweeping across my abdomen to my back, her nails lightly scraping.

She laughs as I tug her leggings off, dragging her down the bed with each pull. Now that she's naked, on my bed exactly where I want her, I'm never letting her leave.

Everything but her slips from my focus as I settle between her hips once more and kiss her lips. She moans against me before stiffening, our kiss breaking suddenly. "What's wrong?" I pull back to look at her face.

"You don't hear that?" Her eyebrows furrow and her eyes squint as she focuses on a sound.

"Hear what?" I cock my head, trying to hear what she's hearing. It's not coming from down the hall from Harrison's room but from the living room. A low buzzing noise accompanied by a chime. "It's my cell," I say with a relieved sigh knowing I'm not on call. "Ignore it."

Her small hands knead the back of my neck and that single touch drives me wild. "Are you sure? What if it's important?"

"Not as important as this." I push any thought of the phone call from my mind with the gentle touch of her lips. Hazel begins to melt against me, the sound of the phone ringing dying in the background.

"Grant?" Hazel's voice is breathless. "It's ringing again."

With a groan, I bury my face in her amazing breasts before sitting up. "Don't move."

Both phones, work and personal, are sitting on the coffee table, and based on the ring alone, it's not work. Frustrated, I snatch the offending phone from the table, answering it with an angry jab. "Wells, what's up?"

"Tristan's got a fever."

In an instant, the anger and frustration dissolves. There's only a handful of things that could pull me from the woman currently lying naked in my bed, but this is one of them. "How high?"

I listen carefully as Wells describes his son's illness taking into account my nephew's medical history. I've been his doctor since the moment he was born and both Wells and myself don't trust anyone else with his well-being, especially with everything my friend has been through. I don't want to see him go through that again.

By the time the phone call ends, I'm already reaching for my keys dreading the fact that I have to leave.

Chapter Eight

Hazel

"I hate to do this, but I have to leave."

It's only been a couple of minutes since he left to answer his phone, but everything about him has changed. His hair's still ruffled from my hands combing through it, but the look in his eyes has turned serious. Concern has me sitting up and reaching for my clothes. "Is everything okay?"

"It's Tristan." He rubs his forehead. "He's sick and Wells is concerned." Grant dresses quickly before cupping my face in his hands. "I wouldn't go if I didn't have to."

"You absolutely have to go." There's no hesitation behind it. If my nephew were sick and my sister called me for help, I'd be out the door in a heartbeat.

"I'm sorry." He leans down to kiss me. "Could you stay here with Harrison? I can call Cole—"

"Go. I'll be here when you get back." I mean every word.

He kisses me again, not a quick peck on the way out the door, but one filled with care and longing. "I love you. I'll be back soon."

Each time those words leave his lips I'm left stunned. Not only did I somehow manage to snag the hottest man on the planet, but he *loves* me.

Me.

I watch him leave, waving at him from the doorway before I head back inside. This isn't how I saw our evening going, but a sick kid is far more important than what we had planned.

Now that we've finally taken the steps to introduce me into their daily lives, things come fast. We go from playing at the park to me watching him while his dad is gone in a single day.

Alright, it might not be that big of a deal—according to Grant he should sleep all night— but something inside my chest is gnawing away at me.

It's not a big deal, I remind myself. *It's for a couple of hours tops. Harrison's asleep. He won't even know I'm here.*

This is the first time I've been to his house since we started dating so I'll take what time I have to do some snooping. We meet at my apartment when we can because it's easier when Grant has to drop Harrison off anyway. The house is a charming two-bedroom with a large open living room leading into a galley-style kitchen. It's nice and lived-in, lacking a feminine touch, but comfortable.

Trying to get my mind off the weight of invisible responsibility, I walk around the living room looking at pictures. It's clear that Grant loves his friends and family, their pictures line the built-in shelves around the fireplace. One in particular stands out.

A young Grant, maybe around Harrison's age, holds a fish, looking up at a distinguished older man in green fishing waders. I'm guessing it's from an infamous camping trip. I wonder if this is the same trip that he had to get stitches from when a hook snagged in the back of his neck.

I'll have to ask him about it later.

There's a whole corner of the living room dedicated to Harrison's toys. Cars, trains, and robots litter the floor with nearly empty toy baskets dumped on their sides.

After all the things Grant does, the least I can do is clean a little. I know he's tired when he gets home from work and coaching, and staying up late to talk with me doesn't help. Sometimes all we can manage is a quick phone call with interruptions of him telling Harrison to clean up and get ready for bed. I guess tonight was one of those nights Grant didn't feel like messing with it.

It takes roughly two minutes to put the toys back in their bins and set them against the wall. I know it's a small thing, but I don't want him coming home after helping Tristan and hurting himself by stepping on something.

After looking around a bit more, I make myself comfortable on the couch. A large yawn cracks my jaw and tiredness creeps in. Before he left Grant told me to make myself at home and I was welcome to sleep in his bed, but it feels weird without him here. So instead of closing my eyes, I pull out my phone killing time until Grant comes home.

The worn brown leather has warmed against my skin and I snuggle deeper into the fluffy *Cars* blanket. It's been a while since Grant left and my eyes grow heavier with each minute.

Determined to stay awake until Grant gets home, I push myself out of the warm cocoon I created on the couch and head for the shelves to browse through his books. Volumes line the shelves and I run my fingers along their spines as I read their titles.

Only to grimace.

All non-fiction medical books. Go figure. Those would put me to sleep faster than a Benadryl.

My heel digs into the carpet as I turn to head back to the couch when I hear it. Faint cries slip from behind Harrison's door and I freeze. Grant said he'd be asleep for the night.

He can't be awake, can he?

Shit.

It's one thing to babysit my nephew, but to be at my boyfriend's house with his son who barely knows me? Yeah, I'm scared of how he'll react, but I can't let a five-year-old cry all alone.

Light-footed, I shuffle down the carpeted hallway and come to a stop outside what I assume to be Harrison's room. Sure enough, hiccuping sobs come from within and I suck in a steadying breath before twisting the knob and glancing in.

"Da-ddy?"

The sobs are gut-wrenching and I wish his dad was here to comfort him, but he's stuck with me, poor guy.

"It's Hazel, Mason's aunt. Do you remember me?" There's not a lot of light in here, but a night light glows on the wall next to his bed, so I inch closer not wanting to frighten him.

"Where's m-my Daddy?" Harrison sits up in bed, little hands wiping the stream of tears from his face. He doesn't seem scared of me, so I carefully perch on the foot of his bed.

I make sure to keep my voice low and calm. The last thing I need is to freak us both out more than we already are. "He had to go take care of Tristan. He should be back soon. What happened?"

At my question, fresh tears begin to fall. I might not be the most motherly person, but I can tell when a kid needs a hug, so I hold open my arms letting him decide whether or not he wants one.

Without hesitation, Harrison crawls into my embrace, burying his head in the crook of my neck, his little arms squeezing tight around me. His little body shakes, his chest heaving as he sucks in gasping breaths.

"You're okay," I whisper, rubbing my hand in soothing circles on his back. "You're okay." I'm not sure if I'm talking to him or myself.

Something close to panic settles in my chest. These are the situations Candice talks about that I don't know what to do. I'm not trained, hardwired, prepared, whatever, for *this*.

All that goes through my head as I continue to do my best to comfort him, is that someone else should be doing this. I'm not qualified. Anyone else is better suited to comfort a crying child than me.

As we sit in the dim light of his bedroom, Harrison's heaving sobs turn into soft hiccups. Little fingers play with a strand of my hair as he calms down. I feel so out of place like I'm doing everything wrong. "You ready to lay back down?"

"No." His arms tighten around me.

Okay then.

"Um, do you want to go wait for your dad in the living room? I saw a very comfy blanket we could cuddle under." I chuckle at his enthusiastic nod.

Harrison's heavier than he looks. For someone so small, it feels like I'm carrying a bag of cement rather than a child. He's clinging to me like a koala, his legs wrapping around my waist the moment I stand. When I try to set him on the couch, he refuses to disentangle his limbs from around me, instead clinging tighter to me.

What do I do now?

I stare awkwardly at the couch debating the best move. He doesn't want down, but I can't stand here all night. Not unless I want my arms to fall off.

Bending my knees to avoid being choked, I grab the blanket, balancing Harrison with one arm to toss pillows where I want them, and head for the corner of the sectional. This way I can have my head and neck supported and use the pillows as armrests.

Plus, the corner is the best seat of a sectional and I'll die on that hill.

Harrison doesn't make a peep as I adjust the blanket over us, but I know he's awake from the slight pulling sensation coming from the hair he's twirling in his fingers.

A deep sense of calm settles through me the longer we sit in the quiet and I let out an involuntary sigh. When Harrison does the same I can't help but let out a small smile.

Time slips by slowly, my mind wandering as Harrison's breathing evens. Sitting here with Grant's son sleeping in my arms, I'm forced to think about things I've been pushing to the sidelines.

Like the fact that I'm dating a single dad and I'm not even sure I want kids. Maybe it's not that I don't want them, per se, but more like I'm not sure how I'd handle it all. Having a whole little person relying on you to take care of them, feed them, and keep them safe...It's a lot. I look at my sister and wonder how she balances it all. How she doesn't crush under the weight of the responsibility of motherhood.

I can't imagine myself in her shoes.

There's no way I can keep up.

I'm not sure I have what it takes to be a mother. I'm not Candice. I can't patch up a boo-boo with a kiss. I can't even comfort a crying child properly. All I've done is hold Harrison and tell him his dad would be home soon. Nothing about this says mother material.

All my internal ramblings and turmoil take up so much of my brain power that I don't even register Grant's back.

Keys clack against the countertop startling me and I squeeze Harrison tighter. "Sorry," Grant whispers, "I thought you'd be asleep." His blue eyes are puffy, his face gaunt from lack of sleep. It's late and we're both exhausted. With heavy steps he walks towards the couch leaning down and kissing me softly before whispering, "He woke up?"

"Yeah," I yawn. "I think he had a nightmare. He wouldn't let me put him down." Grant lowers himself to sit next to me, his hand resting on mine where it's placed on his son's back, and laying his head on my shoulder letting out an exhausted sigh. "How's Tristan?"

"Got his fever down, but it took a while. I'll stop by tomorrow morning to check on him." Exhaustion weighs heavy on him, on all of us. He kisses my shoulder. "Let's go to bed."

Grant carefully unwinds his son from around me, lifting him easily into his arms, but not before giving me another quick kiss. Even when he's bone tired after a long night and with his sleeping child in his arms, he's still making me feel special.

Loved.

I wait for him in the hallway as he puts his son back to bed. He said we're going to bed, but I don't know if he meant alone.

When Grant emerges from Harrison's room he wraps me in a warm hug. I cling to him, wrapping my arms around his waist and letting myself bask in his love. "Thank you," Grant sighs, his lips pressing against my head. "For being here. For taking care of Harrison. You have no idea how much you mean to me."

Something in the softness of his voice has tears stinging my eyes. I pull back looking up into his tired face. "You're welcome." He kisses me, this time without the obstacle of his sleeping son. I must look like a hot mess, but he manages to make me feel like the most beautiful girl in the world.

"Come to bed."

I offer to drive myself home, but Grant won't hear it. There's no way he's letting me drive home this late and this tired. This protective streak in him leaves me swooning. I never imagined someone caring about me so much, loving me so much.

He sets out toiletries for me and lays out one of his t-shirts for me to sleep in. I've seen him shirtless and in bed many times, but watching him go through his nightly routine feels intimate. What we have is far more than a handful of dates and crazy chemistry.

Lifetimes are built on what we share.

Dressed in only his almost too tight shirt, I crawl into his bed feeling a sense of security in him that I've never had before.

He pulls me against his chest, our bodies pressed together from shoulder to hips. Wrapped in his warm embrace, I can't help but think about how his son clung to me and the emotions that brought up.

I'm secure about him. I'm not so sure about myself.

"Grant?" His whispered name lingers in the silence of the room.

Warm lips press against my neck. "Hmm?"

It's not the time to bring this up. It's late and we're both tired. "Never mind."

Grant sighs heavily against my neck before tightening his hold around me and slipping back into sleep.

THE BLUE DINOS SOCCER team has made it to the end of their soccer season and in typical Candice fashion, she's gone all out. Not only have she and Tony set up a canopy, but they've also tied up a large blue banner complete with the team name and colorful dinosaurs. Inside parents set up tables stocked with snacks and set out individualized bags of goodies for each boy.

All I brought was a measly chair.

And now it's back, that feeling that's been lingering. It's never really gone away. Every time there's a quiet moment it flashes in my mind like a neon light: Not Mother Material.

How can such a simple thing as watching my boyfriend's kid for a night set me off like this?

If I'm honest with myself, I know exactly why. It's not just that he's a kid I was babysitting. He's *Grant's* kid. It brought up my biggest insecurities and I don't know how to deal with it.

What's worse is that I don't know how to bring this up to Grant.

It's not something we've talked about. We've talked about a lot of serious topics, but kids never came up. Why would we talk kids when I'm in love with a man who has one? They're a package deal.

"There you are." Candice walks out from underneath the canopy wrapping me in a quick hug. "I was hoping you'd be here."

Grant's on the field watching the boys kick a ball around and I take a moment to look at him. He's so handsome with his tanned legs in black shorts and a white t-shirt, his light brown hair sticking out of a black ball cap. Yeah, I'd say I hit it out of the ballpark with this one.

He spots me, a toothy grin splitting his face as he gives me a quick wink.

After my official introduction to Harrison, Grant and I have been more open about our relationship, but I haven't had the time to tell Candice and I'm not sure that right now is the time.

"It's his last game of the season, of course I'm here. Where's Tony?" I spot Wells and Cole by the player's bench, but my brother-in-law is nowhere to be seen.

She guides me under the shade taking a seat in her folding chair before pulling out a bag of balloons. "Mom and Dad are coming so he went to get extra chairs from the car. Here." She hands me a dozen balloons. "Blow these up."

"What is this? A rave?" I laugh, stretching out the neck of a yellow balloon before placing it in my mouth and blowing.

Candice chuckles. "It felt like we were missing something and I remembered I had balloons in the car that we forgot about for Mason's birthday. I think it'll be a nice touch."

How in the world does she do all of this? I don't think I'll ever understand.

There it is. That tiny little piece of me that wonders whether or not I'd make a good mother. Whether or not I even want kids. Want the responsibility and the lifestyle change. Hell, at times I don't feel responsible enough for just me, how could I take care of a child?

I push it to the back of my mind, choosing to focus on Mason and Harrison and cheering on all their hard work. During halftime, Candice gives me the side-eye when Grant asks me to hold onto his water bottle. I can feel the hole she's drilling into the side of my head with her stare, but I ignore her.

Not the time.

The game ends with roaring applause accompanied by enthusiastic cheers. Pride swells for the team's hard work—they've come a long way since their first game. The boys run around hugging each other until they're piled together in the middle of the field, only breaking away to run through the bridge their families make.

Candice takes over, ushering them all to her canopy to grab their personalized gifts. Watching her command ten five-year-olds, I'm even more dumbfounded by her seeming perfection.

A familiar arm settles across my shoulders and my arm wraps around his waist instinctively. "Are you ready to retire, coach?"

"More like take a much-needed break. I've got other important things to spend my time on." Warm lips press to my temple, the bill of his hat brushing against the top of my head.

"Important things, huh?" I can't help but smile up at him. He's making it clear that I'm a priority and my heart soars. Right before it crashes to the ground in a heap of smoke and dust. "Don't freak out, but my mom's coming over here."

"Are you talking to me, or yourself?" I can hear the smile in his voice, but this situation is less than thrilling.

I suck in a steadying breath. "Both."

This was bound to happen sooner or later. Especially with how close I am to my family. I've never had a relationship reach the point of formally introducing my parents to someone I'm dating. Middle and High School flings don't count—they had to know about them to drop me off at the mall so we could hang out. This is unfamiliar territory and I don't know what to expect.

It's clear that Lynn Bryant is where Candice got her athletic build and winning smile. The one thing I managed to inherit from her is my wild mane. Hers is more tame and elegant, more Greek Goddess to my Medusa, with classy streaks of silver sparkling like glitter in the sunlight. "Grant, it's nice to see you again."

I want to die.

She offers her hand and Grant loosens his hold around me, giving my back a reassuring rub before shaking her delicate hand. "Likewise. Did you enjoy the game?"

Although her eyes are blocked by stylish sunglasses, I can feel the weight of her gaze on me. "I loved it. Mason's come a long way since the start of the season."

All this small talk is going to kill me.

Grant hooks his arm around my waist, pulling me closer to him. He's making it clear that we're a couple and I'm both elated and terrified. As much as I want to be with him, I need to sort out this mess going on in my head.

"Um, do you need help carrying things to the car?" I don't see Tony in the crowd of people celebrating the end of the season and I'll use any excuse to get away from this conversation.

Mom dismisses me with a wave of her hand. "We can get it later." She tilts her head curiously, offering a warm smile before she goes for the kill. "This is new." She gestures at us, her voice full of hopeful curiosity.

"Here we go." The whispered words slip from my lips only loud enough for Grant to hear. He chuckles softly.

We've talked about my family and if there's one thing I wanted him to know, it's that they are always up in my business. There are some things I'd rather keep private, at least for a while. I have no problem being seen with him, or being with him, but I know that I'll be fielding questions for the foreseeable future.

To my eternal gratefulness, Cole confidently strides over, a wiggling toddler in his arms. "Grant, where are the medals?" The little girl squeals, determined to break free from her father's grasp. "Parents are asking."

Grant smoothly excuses himself to grab the missing medals from his car leaving me alone with my mother. "I should go help Candice..."

"Not so fast." The stern mother tone has me scrunching my face and pausing my steps.

"Yes?"

"When were you going to tell us about this?"

"I mean, eventually? Candice doesn't even know."

"Candice doesn't even know, what?" Like a demon who's summoned by the simple utterance of their name, my sister appears, casually drinking from her water bottle.

"What is this, *Maury*?" Neither of them seem to understand my humor. Not even a hint of a smile. "Alright, fine," I give up with a sigh. "I've been seeing Grant for several months."

Candice shrugs nonchalantly. "Tell me something I don't know."

Mom clicks her tongue. "You knew the whole time and didn't tell me?"

"What do you mean, '*she didn't tell you*'? She didn't tell *me* and it's my relationship."

"You haven't been very sneaky," Candice explains. "You guys can't stop looking at each other. Plus, Mason says you guys are getting married and that he and Harrison are going to be cousins. He's real excited." She leans in closer, nudging me with her elbow. "Nicely done."

While this isn't a conversation I want to have right now, I can see the humor of it all. "I mean, who could resist all this?" My sister and I laugh at my little joke but mom stands unfazed.

Mom clears her throat. "I'm still wanting to know how this all happened."

"I'm sure she'll tell us all about it later, Mom," Candice says, saving me from an awkward, embarrassing conversation. "I came to tell you that Mason's been looking for you."

Immediately Mom's whole demeanor changes. "Oh, where is he?" Mom can't resist her grandchildren and goes to quickly find Mason.

Nothing makes me happier than dodging the mother bullet and I breathe a small sigh of relief that it's all over. For now at least.

We follow behind Mom when Candice turns her attention to me. "Don't think that you're going to get away with not telling me. I've been *dying* for you to finally bring it up."

We reach the small group of parents and players gathered in a circle as Grant sorts through the box full of medals.

My sister issues one last reminder before the awards begin. "Remember, this isn't over."

Like I could forget.

Chapter Nine

Hazel

Why am I so nervous? It's not like I've never had a serious conversation with my sister over dinner, but tonight's different.

My worries about kids and my ability to be a mother, let alone a stepmother, haven't gone away. They've been lingering in my mind, popping up to the surface at the most inconvenient times.

Grant's started to notice too. Since soccer season is over, we decided to take Harrison to the zoo. We're trying to be more intentional about the time we spend together, and it was a lot of fun spending time with just the three of us. Grant and I strolled hand-in-hand with an excited Harrison rushing ahead of us. So much of that day was everything I dreamed it'd be.

Except when Harrison fell face-first toward the concrete.

Luckily, he caught himself, managing to scrape his palms and not his whole face. I just stood there as the poor kid cried, not knowing if I should comfort him or leave him alone. Grant was there, calm and prepared, and cleaned the cuts before putting on a cartoon band-aide. Harrison was back to normal five minutes later.

But I wasn't.

A normal person would've clucked and hovered over him to make sure he was okay. Not watching silently over his dad's shoulder gnawing her lip unsure of what to do.

Once we were back on the path to the hippos, Grant offered his hand again and I reluctantly took it. I could see the confusion in the tightness of his eyes, but he didn't say anything. As if he could sense something was off, he simply rubbed his thumb across the back of my hand offering his support.

He makes it so easy to love him.

Which is why I should be an adult and bring this up to him. But instead, I'm cowering out of fear.

If I can't be what Grant wants, will I lose him?

It's that fear simmering underneath my skin.

Candice has been eyeing me the whole time we waited for our table and now that we're seated, I feel like I'm being interrogated by the FBI complete with the pendant lights shining right on me. The way she squints her eyes at me across the table has me quivering in my seat like a scorned child and I haven't even done anything yet. "So Grant, huh?"

After being so intimidated by her, the question makes me snort out a laugh. "Are you upset?"

"Upset? Are you kidding me? I'm downright proud. I've just been waiting for you to finally fess up. Now, tell me everything."

My stomach erupts into butterflies as I tell my sister everything starting from the very beginning. All the nerves I had going into this evening fade away the more I talk. Hearing her gasp and squeal like a teenager as I recount how Grant and I got together, I'm reminded of how lucky I am to have a sister like her. Not every girl has this close of a friendship with their sibling, let alone their older sister. We managed to fight our way through childhood, build an understanding through our teenage years, and foster a close friendship into adulthood.

"So why did you keep it a secret?" she asks as she takes a bite of salmon.

I sigh into my plate. "I don't know. Maybe I thought if I told someone about it, it wouldn't happen. That it would turn out how every other date has. For all I knew, it would be a repeat of Randy."

Candice nearly chokes on her water. "Oh my gosh, I forgot about Randy!"

"I wish I could forget!" I laugh. "I have you to thank for that one." Randy was one of her infamous set-ups. He was a friend of a friend who lived forty-five minutes away in the small town of Rose Prairie. We talked on the phone a few times and I was excited to meet him. Drove to a cute little diner only to find out that Randy was already married. Candice's match-making services were revoked on the spot.

"But seriously, things are good, right?" She asks when our laughter dies down. "You're in love with him. He's in love with you. It's easy to see how much you care for each other. It's written all over your faces when you're together."

I'm not sure how to answer her question. It's not a simple yes or no. Yes, we love each other. Yes, we care very deeply for one another. Yes, things are good. But there's still a but.

Her expression turns serious at my quiet contemplation, concern painted across her face. "Things aren't good?"

If there's any person other than Grant to talk my feelings through with, it would be my sister. She's done all of it: dating, marriage, and parenthood. So why is it so hard to say the words?

"Grant's great. Amazing. He's the guy I've always wanted..."

"But?"

"But," I suck in a large breath holding it for a second before exhaling the words in a rush, "What if I'm not everything he wants?"

Candice softens, smiling at me. It's not meant to chastise but to empathize. "Hazel."

"I know," I mutter through a throat thick with emotion. A headache starts to form from the effort to hold back tears. The middle of a crowded restaurant is *not* the place to have an emotional breakdown.

"Has he said anything to make you think that?"

My answer is quick. "No. Never. Grant's in. A hundred percent. There's nothing about him that I question. It's me that's the problem."

"Okay," she says, placing her fork down. "Help me understand. You love him. You're secure in your relationship with him." I nod. "He's not making you doubt anything, but you're doubting yourself?" I nod again. "Don't take this the wrong way Hazel, but what could you possibly doubt yourself about?"

God this feels like a therapy session. But bottling up these thoughts and feelings isn't doing me any good. If anything, it's putting my relationship in jeopardy. "I just don't know if I can do it."

"Do what?"

"Be a mom."

There it is. The words I've kept hidden and tucked away are out in the open.

Candice's eyes widen as the realization hits. Whatever it was she thought I was going to say, clearly, this wasn't anywhere near what she was thinking. She blinks slowly. "Wow."

An invisible weight has been lifted off my chest at my admission, but that doesn't make the words any easier. "Yeah."

With impeccable timing, the waitress comes by to check on us. I've been pushing the food around my plate and when she offers to take it, I don't hesitate.

"You know," Candice chimes in before our waitress leaves, "I'm thinking we need some chocolate. Split a lava cake with me?" She doesn't even wait for my answer before placing the order.

"You in desperate need of chocolate?" I force a laugh trying to ease the tension. Dessert at a restaurant is normally a special occasion situation.

"Oh this isn't a 'me' thing, it's a 'we' thing. *We* need gooey chocolatey deliciousness." I won't argue with her on that. She takes a long drink of water. "I'm ready to listen when you're ready to talk."

She isn't going to let this go, and if I were her, I wouldn't either. You can't just drop a bomb like that and not elaborate.

"I don't know, Candice. What if I wasn't supposed to be a mom? What if I was always only supposed to be the fun aunt who has responsibility for a short time frame? Be the fun aunt, load 'em up with chocolate and caffeine before sending them home to their parents. I don't know the first thing about raising a kid, or taking care of one, let alone how to keep one alive."

"First, next time you watch Mason we'll make it a sleepover so you have to deal with the ramifications of your sugar-doping actions." A genuine laugh bubbles up my throat. "Second, not for one second do I think that you were only meant to be a fun aunt. You are a fun aunt, but you are so much more than that. You know how to raise a kid because you already help with Mason. You teach him just as much about how to be a good human being as Tony and I do. Keeping a kid alive is a whole other thing," she shakes her head. "But Hazel, I think you'd be a great mom."

How is she able to flip everything upside down? Everything that I've been telling myself for weeks, she blows right through in seconds.

I shake my head. "It still doesn't change how I feel."

The waitress places the dessert in the middle of the table and my mouth waters. Chocolate cake topped with ice cream dribbling down the sides covered in hot fudge. Yum.

Candice scoops out a mouthful of cake. "How does Grant feel about all this?"

I laugh ironically picking up my spoon, stabbing the cake and watching the chocolate ooze out. "I haven't told him."

If looks could kill, I'd be dead. "Hazel," she scorns. "How have you not told him about this?"

"What's he supposed to say? It's not like he can change anything. He's a *dad* and that's never going to change."

Candice thinks around a bite of cake. "How do you know what he's going to say if you haven't told him? Has he said anything to make you doubt that you wouldn't be a good mother?"

I shake my head. "No."

"Then what is it? Why are you putting all this stress on yourself?"

The question is simple but the answer isn't.

"What if I mess up? What if I do or say the wrong thing? I don't know how to be a mom."

Candice forces laughter. "I hate to break it to you, but no one knows how to be a mom. Most of the time, you make it up as you go and hope you don't screw the kid up in the process." She shoves a dollop of ice cream in her mouth. "You probably will screw up at some point. But, then again, that's also the beauty of motherhood. It's joy, heartache, pain, mistakes, forgiveness, growth, love—so much love," she smiles. "I'm not saying it'll be easy or that it's for everyone, but no one's asking you to be perfect."

I know what she's saying is true, but still doubt lingers. "How do you handle it all?"

She laughs like I've told the funniest joke she's ever heard. "I don't. I'm not even close to perfect. Tony would be more than happy to share all my shortcomings," she snorts. "Talk to Grant. Let him know what you're feeling. Maybe it'll ease all this worry."

Just talking with Candice has helped take off some of the heaviness I feel. But she's right. The only person who can help with this is Grant, but it's a conversation I'm scared of.

"Are you going to eat the whole thing or are you going to save some for me?" Candice has been shoveling cake, fudge, and ice cream into her mouth only taking a breath to help ease my concern.

"Fine," she says around a mouthful, "I'll let you have the last bite." But she doesn't stop dipping her spoon in for another mouthful. "But you're going to feel bad when I tell you my secret."

"What secret?"

LOVED BY THE SINGLE DAD

Chapter Ten

Grant

I'm not surprised Hazel wants to talk. There's been something eating away at her for a while now, I just don't know what.

She's gone quiet at times, her gaze fixing on a point and not wavering. That confidence she once harnessed has slipped, moments of self-doubt creeping in that are uncharacteristic for her.

I won't push her to tell me. She'll share with me when she's ready and it looks like now's the time.

All I know is that no matter what happens, she's mine. Nothing will change that.

My parents were more than willing to take Harrison for the weekend. Cole and Wells have been supportive in watching him, but I can see that they both need a break.

Cole continues to struggle with juggling work and the kids. With summer fast approaching, he doesn't know what he's going to do.

Wells, on the other hand, seems to be a ball of coiled tension. With all that he's gone through since Tristan was born, I have a feeling he's going to need to let loose pretty soon. The man rarely takes a moment to relax and is constantly on the move, which makes sense considering everything he's been through. Cole teases him relentlessly, but Wells just brushes him off with a shrug of his shoulders.

I think I need to set up a schedule to watch the kids to give my friends a break.

Hazel's waiting for me as I walk up to her door. She looks stunning as always, her long wavy hair floating loose around her face accentuating her natural beauty. Worry is etched along the tight set of her mouth, only softening as she sighs and steps into my embrace.

"Hey, baby." I kiss the top of her head as she buries her face in my chest, her shoulders relaxing. "Don't tell me your mother grilled you again."

Her shoulders shake with laughter at her new nickname or the question, I'm not sure. When she said she was being a baby about how her mom was acting around us, I told her she was *my baby*. The look of disgust she gave me made us both laugh, but she doesn't seem to mind now.

"I'm sure she would love to try. Is it bad to admit that I've been dodging her phone calls?" Since learning about our relationship, Lynn hasn't let up on gathering information. The pizza party the parents planned after the game was interesting, to say the least. Lynn cornered me whenever she could and I couldn't help but laugh at Hazel's red, embarrassed face.

It's good to see some of the stress melt from her features as she smiles up at me. "Absolutely not." I cup her face and relish the feeling of her lips against mine. I don't let her go easily, pulling her back in again and again for quick kisses and still not getting my fill.

With a soft sigh, Hazel steps out of my embrace and leads me into her apartment.

The scent of lavender is subtle, the flames of the lit candle flickering as I follow Hazel to her couch. I've learned the scent only gets used on certain occasions, and none of them are positive.

"Candice wasn't nearly as bad as my mom," she says as she folds her legs underneath her. Candice had come up to me at the party saying how happy she was for us before tacking on a threat if I should ever hurt her little sister. "She saw right through us, I guess."

"I'm sure it wasn't that hard. I'm an open book when it comes to you. Pretty sure I was watching you more than I was the games." There was no stopping my eyes from wandering over to her. "Hell, I can barely keep my hands to myself right now."

She smiles, rolling her eyes, but offers the hand resting on her thigh which I gladly take. "I'd say my time was evenly split between you and the game. Lucky for me I could watch both at the same time." Her eyes are glued to our clasped hands, her nervousness coming back to the forefront.

It's clear that this is a struggle for her and I'm not going to push her. Instead, I'll sit with her forever if I have to.

She sucks in a deep breath before slowly letting it out through pursed lips. "I don't know why I'm so nervous."

"You don't have to be," I encourage her. "Nothing you say can change my mind about you."

She snickers. "That's why I'm nervous. I feel like this could be the one thing..." She lets her words trail off, her voice thick with emotion.

There's nothing that could make me change my mind, or heart, about her. She's who my life has led me to and I'm not turning my back on what we have.

Ever.

"Nothing you say could make me leave."

The room falls quiet as I give Hazel the space and time she needs to say what she needs to say. Her smaller fingers fiddle with mine as a simple distraction from whatever's going on in that beautiful head of hers.

She breathes heavily, sucking in large inhales before slowly letting them out as if searching for the strength to say the words.

The urge to drag her into my lap and hold her is unmistakable. But instead, I settle for her hand in mine.

When she finally starts to share her thoughts, her voice is soft and timid, unlike the woman I've come to love.

"So, you know that before you I'd been single for a long time." I nod even though her eyes don't move from our joined hands. "There were times that I was fine with that because I would see the stress that having a family did to people and I didn't need it. I'd see my sister with Mason and realize that I'm not that type of girl. I don't know how to be sweet and maternal." She finally looks up at me, her brown eyes pleading.

I have to bite my tongue because although I disagree, this isn't about how I feel about her. She's kind, compassionate, and caring in so many ways that it's mind-boggling that she doesn't see herself that way. So I squeeze her hand letting her know I hear her.

"I thought I would be okay, that it wasn't a big deal. But then Harrison woke up that night and I didn't know what to do. All I could think was that anyone else would've been better than me."

It's hard to keep the disbelief off my face. When I walked into my home that night to see her cradling my sleeping son in her arms, I had never felt so much peace or love. Not once when I was trying to get Tristan's fever down did I worry about Harrison or think that Hazel wouldn't be able to take care of him or keep him safe.

Coming home to her—to them? It was the best feeling I've ever had in my life.

Hazel pauses, sucking in a ragged breath. "I don't know if I can be what you and Harrison need."

All that we need?

She's all that we need.

Her.

Just. Her.

All the breath is stolen from my lungs at the knowledge that she doesn't think she's good enough.

She's *everything*.

"Hazel," I gasp.

"We've never talked about kids, but it's hard not to think about," she rushes. "I know you're already a parent, and Harrison's amazing, but...I'm not sure if I know how to be a mom." She deflates, all the anxiety and worry rushing out with her admission.

With everything out in the open, we sit in the quiet of the living room processing the information she's shared. Hazel squeezes my hand tightly as if she's afraid I'll slip my fingers from hers, walk out that door, and never look back.

Nothing in this world could get me to do that.

I reach over and give her thigh a gentle, reassuring squeeze. "I'm glad you told me. But," I pause, waiting for her to fix her tear-filled gaze on me, "why do you think you won't be a good mom?"

She blinks rapidly looking up at the ceiling before focusing on our clasped hands. "I'm just not...I don't..." She starts and stops, her mouth opening and closing as if she can't find the right words. "I'm not Candice. I don't know how to do all the things. Be all the things."

There it is.

"Baby," I say, scooching closer to her on the couch and tilting her chin up. "I don't want Candice. I *need* you. You are *everything* I need. Everything *we* need. You being exactly who you are is more than enough for us. Even if you doubt yourself, I don't. I've seen you with Mason and with Harrison and never once did I think that you would be a terrible mother."

She sniffles, her eyes filling back up with tears. "What if I mess up?

"Everyone makes mistakes. And if we do mess up, we'll be there for each other and we'll figure it out. I fuck up all the time. We know Cole and Wells have their fair share of mistakes," she hiccups a chuckle. "You don't have to be anything more than mine. Is that okay? You get to decide what role you want to take when you want to take it."

Hazel bites her lip. "But you're not mad or going to break up with me?" She seems genuinely surprised and now the worry hidden in every line of her face makes more sense.

She expected this conversation to end in heartbreak.

The answer is so simple that I don't have to think about it. "No. Never crossed my mind."

Her eyebrows furrow. "Then what are you?"

"Completely in love with you, now more than ever." Her gaze flicks across my smiling face searching it for a hint of a lie. "Hazel, I'd be more concerned if you didn't think about it. Trust me, I understand what it's like to become a parent overnight." My palm glides along her thigh in comfort.

Hazel's whole body seems to loosen as she exhales, leaning forward to place her forehead against mine. "Thank you," she whispers. "I didn't realize how badly I needed to hear that." She snorts. "I feel so stupid now."

Wild hair tickles my cheeks and I brush it away, tucking it behind her ears before kissing her lips. "You're not stupid. You care. There's a difference." I won't point out how her simply recognizing the fear and talking about it makes her better than some people I know. "Please don't go thinking that you're not everything we need."

Hazel nods, kissing my lips once more. "I love you."

With the heaviness of the conversation dissipating, I finally bridge the gap between us, pulling her into my lap and holding her like I've been longing to. We have the whole weekend, the rest of our lives, for me to show her how much she's loved.

Starting right now.

Epilogue

Three Years Later

Hazel

" *OW!* Ow, ow, ow." My knuckles crack against the unyielding lip of the granite countertop from the force of my grip. Blazing lightning streaks up and down my back, across my hips, and radiates along my abdomen. I mean, I knew it would hurt like a bitch, but *my God*.

A small hand makes comforting circles across my back, soft words of comfort falling on deaf ears. The whole world has focused on the sharp, blinding pain that has me doubled over. Within moments that seem like lifetimes, the pain begins to wane and the dull buzz of the world around me grows stronger.

"It's okay, Momma. You'll be okay. Shh. I know it hurts." Over and over again Harrison's gentle voice repeats the same words, his hands moving over me the same way mine have whenever he woke up from a nightmare, hurt himself, or had a bad day.

Sweat beads on my forehead, my hair sticking to my face and I'm panting like a dog, but at least for now, things seem to have quieted down. "Okay," I gasp, loosening my grip. "I'm okay."

"Can we get her a wheelchair or something?" Joanna talks frantically with the nurse behind the front desk before turning her attention to me. "I told you guys to wait in the car."

Harrison places a hand on my arm and shrugs. "She said she needed to walk. Dad says walking's a good thing."

I nod along with him, focusing on my breathing. My stomach hangs low and heavy and I absentmindedly cradle it, stroking up and down over my tight skin. Just when I thought my belly couldn't get any bigger, it did.

Pregnancy was a planned surprise. No matter how much you plan for it—or try for it—it's still an amazing gift.

I might've been a bit hysterical when I told Grant the news. He, on the other hand, was as calm as a cucumber. But seeing the happy smile and tears of joy as he held the onesie I set out on his pillow the night I told him, is something I'll never forget.

This is the first time either of us get to experience everything that comes with pregnancy and planning for a baby. It's been a beautiful, yet stressful, process. Harrison's beyond excited to be a big brother. He and Grant built the crib last week after it finally came in on backorder.

Believe me, thinking I wasn't going to have a bed to bring my baby home to was threatening to put me into premature labor.

The look Joanna shoots my way makes me laugh. Panicked wide eyes with blonde hair flopping over her forehead on top of the low ache in my belly is too much. We've been best friends for decades and I still can't take her seriously when she looks at me like that.

She sighs, exasperated. "First, I have to come pick you up in a grocery store parking lot because you decided to drive yourself instead of waiting for your husband and now you couldn't do the *one* thing I asked you to do?"

A nurse pushes a wheelchair behind me and helps me settle into it before leading us down the hall towards Labor and Delivery. "I had to come inside at some point."

Contractions have been coming and going all day and according to Google they were Braxton Hicks and I shouldn't be worried about them. Should I have called my *doctor* husband or nurse sister who's done this twice?

Yeah, probably.

But it was time to pick Harrison up from school and I saw no point in asking someone else to do it for me. Any one of them would've dropped what they were doing in a heartbeat, but I didn't want to bother them when I was fully capable of doing it myself.

Getting to the school to pick up Harrison wasn't the problem anyway. Driving home was the issue. It wasn't until we were almost home that things started to get more intense and I had to pull over.

Jo helps me get into the hospital gown and in bed before the nurses hook me up with wires and monitors. Harrison sits in the hospital chair talking on the phone with Grant about what's going on as he drives to the hospital. Well, as much information as an almost nine-year-old can relay.

He's gotten so big in the last several years. He's all gangly limbs and buck teeth, but I love him so much. Thinking about not being his momma has tears brimming in my eyes. I can't imagine life without him or his dad in it. We made it official shortly after we got married. Right there on his amended birth certificate where it says "mother" is the name Hazel Elizabeth Rollins.

He's stuck with me for good.

They both are.

The contractions grow closer and more intense and by the time Grant rushes into the room I'm downright exhausted. His warm lips press to my forehead as he whispers my name, his hands working to brush my hair off my face. "How are you feeling?"

Even exhausted I manage a smile. "Seriously? I'm in unmedicated labor and you're asking me how I'm feeling?"

Grant laughs. "Sorry. I guess I'm still in doctor mode. Can I get you anything?"

"The nurse? I think I'm ready for all the drugs."

Joanna jumps up from her spot beside Harrison. "I'll go get her, and then I can take Harrison." She checks her phone, typing out a quick message before sliding it back into the pocket of her jeans. "Everyone's all set. We'll take Harrison to Grant's parent's house." Harrison groans, clearly wanting to stay with Tristan or Jett. "And your mom and Candice are on their way." Jo squeezes my toes as Harrison gives me a quick kiss before leaving.

I nod, only half listening as another contraction starts to set in. Grant holds my hand through it all being as supportive as he can be.

"Someone's ready for an Epidural?" Nurse Kendra knocks politely on the open door before stepping inside. She's vaguely familiar to me, with long dark braids and a kind smile, but all I can think about right now is getting this baby out of me.

The peak of the contraction starts to wane and I breathe a little easier, but still unable to talk, so my husband does it for me. "Yes. She wanted to wait until I got here, stubborn as she is," he looks over at me and winks.

If I could talk right now, I'd show him how stubborn I could be and where he could shove that wink.

Nurse Kendra flips through papers being fed from a machine hooked to the monitor around my belly.

Grant watches her over his shoulder. "The contractions seem to be happening close together?" Oh, he's gone full doctor mode, asking a question like it's a statement.

Papers rustle beside me as my muscles relax. "Yes, they are. Hazel, how long have you been having contractions?"

Grant's piercing gaze pins me to the mattress. Does it make me a coward if I refuse to look at him? "Um, all day."

"You were having contractions all day?" Rarely does my husband lose his temper, and usually it doesn't last for long because I find it sexy as hell, but this time, it's terrifying.

I fiddle with my fingers resting on top of my giant pregnant belly as Nurse Kendra asks for consent to do a pelvic exam to see how dilated I am. "I was fine. I honestly thought they were nothing," I reassure him as Kendra sets everything up.

Grant grabs my hand bringing it to his lips, the anger gone as quickly as it appeared. "I know, baby."

Kendra talks me through the exam, warning me about the pressure before it happens. Then Kendra says the one thing I absolutely do not want to hear right now. "Hazel, I think it might be time to push."

WE'VE HAD SEVERAL HOURS to ourselves and our new bundle of joy. The whole process of giving birth was a whirlwind. Thankfully Grant was with me every second of the way. He and Kendra talked me through what was happening and helped me get into the most comfortable pushing position.

What would've made me even more comfortable was drugs, but Kendra said it was too late for that. Now I know not to wait all damn day next time.

It's all worth it though.

Lydia's full lips suckle air as she sleeps in my arms, my finger stroking over her chubby pink cheeks. She's absolutely perfect. Ten fingers. Ten toes. Seven pounds and I forget how many ounces. Grant's checked over all her vital signs, even though he hand-selected Doctor Bailey as our pediatrician, the protective dad that he is.

I hear them before I see them. Harrison's a little over-excited and practically yells his questions to his dad as they walk down the hallway. We've kept everyone waiting until the most important introduction could be made first.

"You're about to find out." Grant leads Harrison into the room, his hands clutching his shoulders.

Harrison's green eyes widen as he notices the bright pink blanket wrapped around the newest edition of our family. "I have a sister?"

I hold out a hand to him, careful of the I.V. "Are you gonna come and meet her?"

As I hold my two children in my arms, my husband kissing the top of my head, I've never been more content.

This is everything I need.

Thanks For Reading

Thank you so much for reading *Loved by the Single Dad!*

I usually talk about what inspired each book in this section, so I might as well do that now. Would you believe me if I told you that all this came from attending my real-life nephew's soccer game? I was on the record for trying to be *Aunt of the Year* and it was his first game of the season with a new team (at least I think it was). I was so distracted by the coach—a tan, tattooed, attractive, *married*—man.

Very much like Hazel, I had the same feeling she was having while staring at Grant. "Why is it so attractive?" "Why is he married? They're *always* married." Also like Hazel, I pulled out my phone and texted my best friend. The entire game we were building this idea in my head, forming the SDC and I immediately came home and made the covers. Granted, those were scrapped and remade over and over, but still.

Cole's book *Nanny for the Single Dad*[1] and Wells's book *Desired by the Single Dad*[2] will be coming soon and are up for pre-order now!

If you could, please take a moment to rate and review on Amazon, Goodreads, Instagram, or wherever you post reviews. As an indie author, ratings and reviews are the best way of

---

1.   *https://a.co/d/0h4oOQo*

2.   *https://a.co/d/2k3CbNY*

getting my work out there for other people to read. A little goes a long way!

Don't forget to follow me on Instagram @authorsierrashipley [3]and sign up for my newsletter[4] to get freebies and see more details about my coming books!

Thank you for your support!

Until next time,

Sierra

---

3.   https://instagram.com/authorsierrashipley?igshid=YmMyMTA2M2Y=

4.   https://mailchi.mp/db7893726a2a/sierra-shipley-newsletter-sign-up-page

About the Author

Sierra Shipley is a born and raised Midwest girl. She spends her days with her lovable rescue pup, Trip, who constantly wants all the cuddles, and her lovable cat Aidas. Her ideal day is spent drinking coffee, reading, and dreaming.

Sierra has always wanted the romance she's read in books. Pair that with an active imagination and a love of creativity, and you get a writer!

Sierra wants to create steamy, romantic stories with characters that people can relate to.